'You idiot! Don't ⸻ going?'

The words were ⸻ breath as Kate began to rise and turned to face her attacker.

'*What* did you say?' The dark face above her own was uncompromising.

'I'm sorry if I seemed rude, but honestly it was your own fault, really it was. I hadn't even touched the doors; I was trying to turn round to check that there was no one⸻'

'And no one's ever told you that it's a bloody silly thing to do to back through a door on a children's ward, I suppose?' the man said acidly.

'All right. I'm very sorry you hit me in the back with the doors, causing me to hurl books and toys all over the place,' Kate said bitterly. 'Far be it from me to try to apportion blame!'

'If it makes you happier to believe yourself blame-free at all costs then I won't argue with you,' the man said. He hesitated, then smiled reluctantly. 'If you hadn't shouted at me I dare say I might have acknowledged that I wasn't looking where I was going either. So shall we agree to be more sensible in future? Both of us?'

'All right,' Kate agreed. 'I'll write my bruised knees down to experience.'

He was very nearly grinning, Kate saw. 'That's right. Your wounds will teach you to be more careful.'

Lydia Balmain was born in Norwich, Norfolk, but at the outbreak of war the family moved down to North Devon where they spent the next few years. In 1957 she and her husband Brian, a trading standards officer, moved to Tunbridge Wells in Kent where she worked as a secretary for a construction firm.

After the birth of two sons and two daughters, she began writing in earnest—before then she had written for fun—and in the eighties turned to medical romance, her family having been involved in medicine for a number of years.

Now living in north-west Britain, she does a great deal of research into modern medical techniques and enjoys a good relationship with the staff of her local hospital, who are used to being cross-questioned whenever she needs background material for her books.

Lydia Balmain has four pen-names and is a prolific writer in several genres.

HOMETOWN HOSPITAL

BY

LYDIA BALMAIN

MILLS & BOON LIMITED
ETON HOUSE   18–24 PARADISE ROAD
RICHMOND   SURREY   TW9 1SR

First published in Great Britain 1991
by Mills & Boon Limited

© Lydia Balmain 1991

Australian copyright 1991
Philippine copyright 1991
This edition 1991

ISBN 0 263 77497 X

Set in 11 on 13 pt Linotron Palatino
03-9112-45033
Typeset in Great Britain by Centracet, Cambridge
Made and printed in Great Britain

CHAPTER ONE

'STAFF, when you've finished there could you come along to my office, please? I won't keep you long—I know there's a lot to do, but Freda and Jane can cope for a bit.'

'Yes, Sister, of course,' Kate Reagan said breathlessly. As Sister disappeared through the swing doors into the corridor Kate looked across at Jane, sturdily tucking in covers on the opposite side of the bed. 'It can't be anything I've done wrong, because I haven't been here long enough; wonder what she wants?'

Jane, a third-year student, shrugged.

'Children's wards aren't like the adult ones,' she said. 'We all got a pep talk when we started, but I reckon you'll know all that. Adèle said something about your having trained at one of the big children's hospitals in London, which is why they appointed you, of course. So probably it's just to tell you about ward-rounds and so on.'

'Yes, probably,' Kate agreed. She was a slim girl with soft, fawn-coloured hair pulled back into a pony-tail, a ready smile and a pair of unusually large grey-blue eyes. Now she straightened her dress, checked with a swift

downward glance that her apron was unsullied
and her fob-watch neatly in place, and set off
across Pantomime Ward for Sister Adèle Fox's
office.

As she went she glanced curiously about her,
for this was not only her first day on Pantomime
Ward but her first day in the Elizabeth Hospital
at Colney Bay. The hospital was not modern,
but despite its old-fashioned red brick and
stucco exterior it had been brought as up-to-date
as possible inside, with the children's wards,
Pantomime one, two and three, now as bright
and homely as planning and the money available could make them.

Coming from a big London children's hospital, Kate had been pleasantly surprised to find
that the place she had last seen about eighteen
years ago, as an in-patient having a tonsillectomy, had changed considerably for the better.
Gone the chipped iron cots which struck terror
into the hearts of the young with their decided
similarity to prison cells, gone the décor of green
and brown which, the staff at the time would
probably have said, helped to conceal the
grubby fingerprints of their small inmates.
Gone, what was more, the attitude which found
parents a nuisance and kept them at bay as
much as possible, scolded sick children for
daring to cry or complain and seemed positively
to delight in terrifying the young with the

sudden arrival of trolleys laden with what looked like finely honed instruments of torture.

Instead, Kate saw cartoon-covered walls, beautiful curtains, gay with pictures of much-loved bunnies and teddies, boys' bedspreads with racing cars on them and girls' with ponies and seaside pictures.

It was clear that Sister Adèle Fox was an efficient administrator as well as a much-loved nurse, which would make things easier for Kate, who had taken the job of staff nurse in order that, when Sister Fox left, she might take over as sister of Pantomime Ward.

She was bound to admit, however, as she walked swiftly down the long ward, that it was not a particularly neat and tidy place. There was a large play area next door where, in addition to their normal games and pastimes, the children were encouraged to play at doctors and nurses using old medical instruments, but a great many toys and books still littered the ward. At this time in the morning few of their small patients were actually here, being mostly in the play-room, but those who were still in their beds seemed to be happily occupying themselves.

They're as content as they can be in the circumstances, so this is a good ward, Kate told herself, collecting cast-down toys as she went. Since she was going to the office she might as well tidy on her way. One of the children, returning from the playroom and seeing the new nurse so engaged, came over to help her, piling her arms yet higher until it was all Kate could do to see over the top of them.

'Thank you very much,' Kate said. 'Are you going. . .?' But the child had disappeared, hurrying up the ward, intent on whatever errand had brought her out of the playroom in the first place. Smiling to herself, Kate backed up against the ward doors, resting her shoulders against them and beginning to turn to peer through the glass to make sure no one was attempting to enter. But before she had a chance to do so the doors rammed her hard in the back, shooting her forward so that she and her armful of assorted toys were hurtled halfway up the ward, to land in an ignominious heap on the floor.

Kate was momentarily winded but she began to scramble to her feet, longing to give utterance to the thoughts which were jostling in her mind.

'You idiot! Don't you ever look where you're going?'

The words were out and regretted in the same breath as Kate began to rise and turned to face her attacker. He was a tall man, dark-haired, and right now he was blazingly angry, which seemed unfair, considering who had most definitely been at fault. Kate took another, deeper breath to tell him so, and hesitated. He was, she realised, clad in theatre blue. . .Oh, no, let him be a very junior houseman, she prayed, while uneasily aware that a man who appeared to be in his early forties and who had a decided air of command was unlikely to be still working his way up the medical ladder.

'*What* did you say?' The dark face above her own was uncompromising. Useless to deny her words; Kate, on her feet once more, backed up against the doors and tried a smile. It was not returned.

'I'm sorry if I seemed rude, but honestly it was your fault, really it was. I hadn't even touched the doors; I was trying to turn round to check that there was no one——'

'And no one's ever told you that it's a bloody silly thing to do to back through a door on a children's ward, I suppose?' the man said acidly. 'Suppose a child had been coming through the doors, Nurse? A small child, with a catheter-bag? Do you realise the damage you might have done?'

This was too much! How like a man, particularly a man of his age, to try to foist the blame for an accident on someone else! He had been coming through the doors without looking, but would he admit it? Not he. Some poor little nurse must take the blame. A member of the surgical team, which he clearly was, could never admit that he had caused an accident, particularly one which would have called for the afore-mentioned member of the team to have to unbend and apologise!

'All right. I'm very sorry you hit me in the

back with the doors, causing me to hurl books and toys all over the place,' Kate said bitterly. 'Far be it from me to try to apportion blame!'

'If it makes you happier to believe yourself blame-free at all costs then I won't argue with you,' the man said. He hesitated, then smiled reluctantly. 'If you hadn't shouted at me I dare say I might have acknowledged that I wasn't looking where I was going either. So shall we agree to be more sensible in future? Both of us?'

'All right,' Kate agreed. 'I'll write my bruised knees down to experience.' She started to pick up toys and was pleasantly surprised when he stooped and began to help her. She saw now that he was quite nice-looking, but when, piled up with toys once more, she headed for the doors he pushed them open for her and held them, giving her the slight smile of one who still does not intend to admit a fault.

'That's right. Your wounds will teach you to be more careful.' He was very nearly grinning, Kate saw, and was turning away when he spoke again. 'You're new, aren't you? What's your name?'

'Yes, I started this morning. Staff Nurse Kate Reagan.'

He nodded carelessly. 'Right, Staff. Well, no doubt it will be a lesson to you to look before you leap.'

And with that he was gone, Kate thought crossly, walking gingerly along the corridor to the playroom and decanting her armful of toys off on to a convenient cupboard top. She had told him her name, but he hadn't had the common good manners to reciprocate. Still, she would doubtless discover just who it was she had offended in the fullness of time. And it'll be someone important, she thought dismally, heading once more for Sister's office.

It would be nice if he was a visiting registrar, or a doctor who was usually on another ward, Kate thought as she went on her way. The paediatric surgeon who was responsible for Pantomime Ward was called Charles Patrick, but she had the feeling that he was a much older man. At worst, then, her encounter might have been with his registrar.

Kate glanced down at herself as she walked along. She had skinned the palms of both hands and bruised her knees, but other than that her abrupt fall seemed to have left no marks.

Sister's office was off this corridor, as was the playroom, the television-room, the kitchen and the sluice. The corridor was gaily decorated with cartoon characters—Winnie the Pooh, Tigger and Piglet frolicked on the walls—but Kate scarcely noticed them, for she had reached Sister's office. She tapped lightly, then walked in.

Sister Fox was sitting behind her desk, writing busily, but she looked up as Kate entered and smiled, gesturing the younger girl to a chair. Adèle Fox was a sweet-faced woman in her

forties, who had married late—only the previous year—and was expecting a baby at
Christmas, so wanted to leave as soon as Kate
felt able to take over.

'I've fought for this place,' she said to Kate
now, her round, pretty face wrinkling with
amusement at her own choice of words. 'Oh, it
sounds melodramatic, but it's true. The admin
staff here wanted all sorts of technological
advances, but it's only since Mr Patrick came
that we've managed to get our fair share of
whatever was going. Absalom Jones was a die-
hard of the old school—children should be seen
and not heard; if something was thrown out of
another ward then it would do very well for
Sister Fox's babies. . .' She laughed at Kate's
face. 'Truly, Staff, that's how it's been for years,
until Absalom retired and Mr Patrick took over.'

'What's he like?' Kate asked nervously. When
she had heard talk about the paediatric surgeon
on Pantomime Ward the nurses must have been
referring to old Absalom. That meant, horror of
horrors, that the unfeeling man in theatre
clothes who had bumped into her might very
well have been the up-and-coming Charles
Patrick! But she saw no reason to say anything
to Sister, not at this stage. 'Judging from what
the rest of the staff have said, you either love
him or hate him!'

'He's an extremely able paediatrician and he's
good with children, or at least as good as most

men and a great deal better than Absalom,'
Sister Fox said. 'I won't pretend we haven't had
our disagreements because when you meet him
you'll see why. His medical knowledge and
expertise is not in question, but he hasn't yet
fully acknowledged the parents' role in child-
care, nor the fact that a happy child recovers
quicker than an unhappy one. And, like that of
a good many surgeons, his attitude to babies is
that whatever he does to them is for their
eventual good, so they must put up with the
trifling inconveniences of pain and distress by
themselves, where they won't disturb others.'

'Even the most enlightened surgeons seem to
have similar views,' Kate admitted. 'It's the end
justifying the means, I suppose, but I think even
the tiniest baby benefits from lots of company
and all the consideration possible, whether it
comes from the nurses or from its parents.'

'I quite agree. I believe you were a patient
here in my predecessor's time? There was no
parental popping in and out then, I'll be bound.'

'Not that I can remember. But, since at that
stage I was at the children's home and no one
visited me at all, I'm not a very good judge. My
parents separated when I was only a couple of
years old, so I don't remember an awful lot
about it, but I was six when I came here to have
my tonsils out, and I was a fair way to becoming
institutionalised. I just did whatever I was told

and kept my head down. . .but I was miserably unhappy during the visiting period—I shall never forget that.'

'You poor little thing,' the tender-hearted Sister Fox said, her voice gentle. 'What happened to you? Why weren't you adopted?'

'My mother refused to let me be adopted on the grounds that she intended to have me back, and she wouldn't let me be fostered, either. But when I was seven she remarried, announced she had no further interest in me, and I was fostered.'

'Really? And were you happy?'

'Yes, very happy. But my foster-parents had a son, Don, who emigrated to Australia, and when I was sixteen they decided they wanted to go over there to live as well. They wanted me to go too, but I wasn't keen. By then I knew I wanted to nurse kiddies, and I'd applied for a cadetship at the St James's Hospital for Sick Children. So my foster-parents went, and, though we write and they keep inviting me to stay with them, I've somehow never gone, and I don't suppose I shall now. But perhaps that was why I wanted to come back to Colney Bay so badly, because, although my first seven years here were unhappy, once I was fostered I had a marvellous childhood. And, of course, I did know that I'd only be acting staff nurse until you left, when I'd be made up to sister.'

'And I'm sure you'll be happy here now,'

Sister Fox said robustly. 'It's a delightful place to live and, although perhaps I say it as shouldn't, this hospital is a first-rate one. You'll like the rest of the staff, I hope, and I'm sure you'll love the patients as I do.'

'I'm sure I shall,' Kate agreed. 'Now, Sister, I'm positive you didn't get me in here to talk about my childhood! What did you want to tell me?'

'Well, I wanted to say there would be a ward round in an hour, with Mr Patrick, his registrar, Bob Nettall, and, of course, the students, since this is a teaching hospital. Have you met our current houseman yet?'

'I don't think so,' Kate admitted. 'I only arrived in Colney Bay yesterday, so I haven't had much time to meet anyone. What's his name?'

'It's a woman—Dr Estelle Carruthers. The only thing wrong with Miss Carruthers is that she's the most beautiful thing I've ever set eyes on, and unfortunately not nearly as efficient as she should be, and because she's so adorably pretty she gets away with murder. I've managed to see that she does no real damage, but you have to watch her like a hawk.'

'I'll watch her every move, then,' Kate said, rather amused at the older woman's frankness. 'What sort of a doctor will she make, though, if we cover up her mistakes for her?'

'She'll be dreadful, of course,' Sister Fox said

cordially. 'But the patients have to come first, and, while an adult patient will say to X-ray "it's my left leg that hurts", a child simply accepts that, in the odd adult world, when a left leg hurts the right one gets its picture taken!'

'Right. Then I'll keep an eye on Dr Carruthers,' Kate agreed. 'Anything else?'

'Well, I'm not going to prejudice you against the nursing staff by saying one's more efficient and reliable than another, but do keep your eye on the first-years. They're dear little girls, but subject to human error. In one or two cases, very subject. I won't advise you not to disagree with Mr Patrick, because there are times when he'd try the patience of a saint. You'll just have to see how you get on.'

After that Sister Fox got down to the nitty-gritty of case-notes and patient care, and almost before they knew it there was a knock on the door and the surgical team entered, with a tall man at their head who must be Mr Patrick, Kate realised with a sinking heart. It was, as she might have guessed, her adversary of earlier on.

'Ah, Sister,' the tall man said. 'Ready for the round? As you can see, we're all raring to go.'

'Yes, we're ready,' Sister said. 'Mr Patrick, this is Staff Nurse Kate Reagan. As you know, she's joined us with a view to taking over the job of sister in a couple of months, when I leave.'

'Yes. Staff and I have already met,' Mr Patrick

said coolly, then appeared to relent and gave Kate a wintry smile. 'Unfortunately, with some violence, both of us going through a doorway without checking first that no one was in the way. Are you feeling better now, Staff? No residual bruising, I trust?'

'I'm fine, thank you, sir,' Kate said politely. It looked as though the whole thing would pass over without any more comment, with a bit of luck.

'Good. Then I'll introduce the rest of my team. This is my registrar, Dr Nettall, my houseman, Dr Carruthers. . .' Mr Patrick went rapidly through his team while Kate covertly took stock of both of them and of himself. She had not really noticed him much at the time of their collision, seeing only the height and the anger, but now she looked at him objectively. He was tall, with dark hair cut so short that its tendency to curl was curbed. He had a thin, intelligent face and very dark eyes which, Kate was almost sure, would prove to be blue if one got close enough. His skin was pale, the mouth wide and held in a firm line which indicated that he would not suffer fools gladly. His nose was high-bridged, giving him an arrogant look which a narrow but determined chin did nothing to dissipate.

He caught Kate's scrutiny and, unexpectedly, grinned. It changed his whole face, that sudden, almost boyish expression, softening the dark eyes, revealing good teeth.

'Well, Staff? Taking a good look at what you're up against?'

Kate smiled as well; no point in letting him assume that she was the nervous type! Their previous encounter had upset her somewhat, but when you had had to fend for yourself for years you became not only self-reliant but self-confident too—or went under. Kate had decided long ago that whatever the world flung at her she would meet head on.

'Well, shall we say next time I'll pick on someone my own size?' Kate said with a rueful smile. 'And I'll be more careful as well.'

'Very wise of you, Staff.' Mr Patrick turned towards the door. 'Come along, then, I've got a list this afternoon, you know.'

The whole party swept through into the ward with Mr Patrick leading. Following meekly, Kate thought about the other members of the paediatric team. Dr Nettall was a bit younger than Mr Patrick, probably in his mid-thirties, she thought, but the houseman, beautiful Dr Carruthers, was probably no more than twenty-four or -five—around Kate's own age, in fact. She was every bit as beautiful as Sister Fox had led Kate to believe; a stunning ash-blonde, blue-eyed, curvaceous, she had been very aware that Dr Nettall could scarcely take his eyes off her, and had played up to his admiration by never looking directly at him but letting the long hair fall, veil-like, across her face, whilst she'd made a play with the most carefully manicured hands Kate had ever seen on a member of the medical profession. Her nails, each one a perfect oval, were polished with clear pink gloss, and she paid them a good deal of attention, fiddling with them when no one was looking at her. . . I rank as no one, Kate thought. Dr Carruthers had given the new staff nurse the merest glance in passing, accompanied by the slight smile which Kate knew to be less a greeting than a summing up; the other girl was deciding whether or not Kate constituted either a threat or competition and, Kate knew from experience, she would then adjust her attitude accordingly. Awful to be young, lovely to look at and predatory, Kate thought, but that just about summed up the attitude of the beautiful doctor to her fellow women.

'And how are you feeling this morning, young man?'

They had stopped beside the first occupied bed. Kate glanced at the chart at the foot of it, and at the small brown face of the occupant— Rhajit Singh, aged seven.

'And who will tell us about this youngster?' Mr Patrick's eyes swivelled hopefully around the group. 'How about our newest recruit— Staff?'

'As it happens, I know Rhajit has had a

tonsillectomy, which gave some trouble post-operatively,' Kate said diffidently. It was unfair to ask her when she had scarcely been on the ward two hours, but that was surgeons for you; she did not think for one moment that he was still punishing her for their unfortunate collision! Her eyes flickered down to the boy's chart and she thanked her stars for excellent long sight. 'However, the bleeding was of short duration, Rhajit has been drinking lots and lots, and should be able to go home tomorrow before lunch.'

'Hmm. Well done. Yes, Rhajit, Staff is quite right, you'll be off home tomorrow if all goes according to plan. No school, either, for the rest of the term. Like school, do you?'

'It's all right,' Rhajit said. He gave Mr Patrick a toothy smile. 'I'm jolly clever, you know—top of the class in maths, even if my writing is wobbly.'

There was a general laugh and the group moved on to the next occupied bed.

'Atrial septal defect,' Sister Fox whispered, drawing Kate to one side. 'Nice little girl— Alison Bailey—come in for pre-op treatment. She'll need a lot of care. Mother will stay with her after the op, and possibly just before it as well, but she has three other children and it's a one-parent family. . . Dear me, the distress a broken marriage causes when a child has an extended stay in hospital! If only young people thought a bit longer before jumping into commitments.'

'When will she have the op?' Kate whispered back. 'Just in case Mr Patrick decides to cross-question me again.'

Sister shrugged.

'We don't know yet, but Mr Patrick won't do any hole-in-the-heart type operations until the child's at a fitness peak, so we're building her up, getting her confidence. She's a middle child, always more difficult to nurse in my experience, though why that should be I'm not altogether sure.'

The group round the bed finished their discussion of the girl's case and moved on once more, Kate with them. Dr Nettall moved nearer to Sister Fox and gave Kate a conspiratorial wink. He was a short, stocky young man with a friendly smile and blond, badly-cut hair.

'You did well, Staff. Odd that Mr Patrick asked you anything, knowing you were new today. Still, you certainly took it in your stride, and you'll soon fit in with Adèle here to hold your hand.'

'Yes, she will,' Sister Fox murmured. 'Ah, the next patient is Suzy. . .we may have some trouble here.' She hurried ahead of them to the next bed where a young girl lay. A tangle of red hair almost obscured her face, but what was visible looked sulky.

'Suzy's on traction, I see,' Kate said, since Dr

Nettall was still standing beside her, a little back from the group round the bed. 'What's she done?'

'Fractured pelvis,' Dr Nettall said briefly. 'She's only eleven, despite looking quite fifteen, and desperately difficult to nurse. She was in the orthopaedic ward for a bit but they brought her here after Sister Granfall said she couldn't cope. And your boss. . . Adèle. . .does wonders, I must say. No parental back-up, of course. Eldest child, half-a-dozen younger ones to worry about, out-of-work father, shiftless mother . . .oh, yes, you've got your work cut out to keep young Suzy from turning the whole hospital upside-down, let alone Pantomime Ward.'

'All right, Suzy; I'll bring Staff Nurse Kate to see you properly when the ward round's over,' Kate heard Sister Fox whisper to the patient as the group moved on. 'In the meantime just lie quiet, there's a good girl.'

The 'good girl' looked rebellious, but Kate, moving on with the rest, flashed her a sympathetic smile. It was tough on Suzy being in a ward with so many younger children, and being confined to bed as well. She knew that a lot of hospitals would have insisted that the child stay on orthopaedics, however, and told herself approvingly that this just showed that the Elizabeth was a cut above the rest so far as understanding and sympathy for the patients went.

And presently, the ward-round over, she was able to go back to Sister's room and learn, in far greater detail, about the occupants of Pantomime Ward.

When the briefing was over, though, Sister did not seem in any hurry to let her newly acquired staff nurse return to her duties.

'Now, Kate, I believe you're living in the nurses' home for the time being, but I imagine you'll want a place of your own once you decide to stay. Have you given any thought to a move?'

'Not really,' Kate confessed. 'It seemed a bit premature, since I only arrived in the town yesterday!'

'Well, if you are interested, I happen to know someone with an empty flat. One of my friends has a very large house which she's divided into three, and the garden flat is empty. Normally it would be rather expensive for one person, particularly on a nursing wage, but as it happens Maria is anxious to get someone reliable, and will accept a nominal rent just for the companionship, and for someone to do the garden. Are you fond of gardening?'

'I haven't done much,' Kate admitted. 'But this does sound interesting—tell me more!'

'Well, Maria is Italian, she married an Englishman several years ago and came to live here in Colney Bay. She and her husband were happy here, they have two small children and a couple of cats. . .and then, two months ago, Ralph got seconded to America for a year. The eldest child, Sasha, has just started school and Maria did not want her education interrupted, so she's stayed behind. But she's nervous in that big house, alone except for the kids, and she thought she'd fill the garden flat at least. It's a delightful flat—Ralph converted one wing of the house into the garden flat and the one above it, which is unoccupied, I believe. The people who had it grumbled about the children and Maria's radio, so when they left she didn't re-let. So, you see. . .'

Kate did. She saw that Sister Adèle Fox was the sort of person who would do anything for a friend, and she guessed that she, too, might find Maria's children noisy and her radio loud. But on the other hand. . .the garden flat!

'It sounds ideal,' she said now, a trifle nervously, to be sure, but still enthusiastically. 'Can I go round, take a look at the place?'

'If you're free we could go round this evening, after work. I'll go with you, introduce you to Maria and so on.'

'That sounds ideal,' Kate said gratefully. 'It's a date!'

CHAPTER TWO

IN THE changing-room Kate swopped her brand-new, starched uniform for a casual cotton dress in a pretty shade of blue, slid her lace-ups off and pushed her feet into high-heeled sandals. Around her the room buzzed with conversation, for the other staff nurses who had been doing the nine-to-five shift were also changing, and were, furthermore, a friendly lot, eager to get to know the new girl.

'So you're off with Sister to see this flat?' Nell, who worked a floor above Kate, on Orthopaedic, said as she tidied her bush of dark curly hair. 'I'm desperately fed up with the nurses' home. . .what are the chances of your wanting a flat-mate?'

'Why don't you come as well, and see whether you'd like it?' Kate said at once. 'I'm sure if Adèle had known you wanted a change she'd have offered it to you first of all; you've surely got a prior claim, I'm so new!'

'I've not been here long, actually, but Sister hopes I'll agree to marry Richard and settle down,' Nell said gloomily. 'It isn't that I'm not fond of him, because I am; it's just that I haven't made my mind up yet that he's the person in the world I most care about. In fact, ever since Adèle and her beloved Fred decided to get married she can't wait to see everyone else follow suit.' Nell laughed at Kate's expression. 'Yes, you'll find she's matchmaking like anything as soon as she's got to know you. . . Is there anyone suitable living in this block of flats she's taking you to see?'

'No, there can't be. The flat above the one I'm seeing is empty,' Kate said thankfully. 'Anyway, if she starts matchmaking for me she's in for a disappointment. I'm a career nurse; I haven't the faintest intention of marrying anyone, no matter how eligible or suitable.'

'That's what we all say until we meet the right man,' someone else said ruefully. She was a thin, energetic girl wearing a wedding-ring, with light hair plaited in a long tail down her back. She smiled at Kate. 'I'm Mandy Davies; I'm a bit further along the corridor than you are, in ENT. You're Kate Reagan, from Pantomime, aren't you?'

'Hello, Mandy,' Kate said. 'Nice to meet you. How did you know who I was, though?'

'Yours is the only unfamiliar face, and Sister Fox boasted about getting a nurse from St James's,' Mandy explained. 'You'd been a staff nurse there for over two years, she said, and she thinks you're an ideal replacement for herself. I hope you'll be very happy with us.'

Kate slung her cream-coloured jacket across

her shoulders and picked up the capacious bag she used.

'Thanks, Mandy, I'm sure I shall. Do you want to come and see the flat, Nell?'

'No, better not. But don't forget—if you fancy a flat-share I'm your man. . .or woman, perhaps I should say.'

Kate agreed to remember Nell and left the changing-room to join Sister, as arranged, in the car park. Adèle was waiting for her, neat in a navy and white cotton dress with her dark hair brushed loose. She looks much younger, Kate thought, and realised that the severity of her uniform, plus having to keep one's hair tied back, could add years to a woman's age.

Adèle turned and saw her.

'Well done; I was afraid that lot would keep you talking half the night,' she said briskly. 'That's my car, the blue Ford Fiesta.'

She unlocked the door, saw Kate into the passenger-seat, and then went and took her place behind the wheel.

'Can you drive?' she asked conversationally as she turned the car out of the park and into the busy promenade. 'I won't pretend it's essential in a place like Colney, but it's certainly useful.'

'No, but I'm going to take lessons,' Kate assured her. 'In London it never seemed to matter, public transport's so good, but here, unless I drive, how can I ever get to see the surrounding countryside? The mountains are so beautiful, and, though I suppose I could get a bus, it wouldn't be the same as going up there in a car and just spending the day walking and exploring.'

'True. And driving's a skill which everyone should possess, even if they don't use it,' Adèle said seriously. 'Not far now.'

They were on the outskirts of the town and still heading towards the distant mountains. Kate felt a stab of doubt. . .where was this flat, anyway? Without a car or the ability to drive one she could scarcely live miles from the hospital in the heart of the country!

But it was all right. They were on a wide tree-lined road with big houses on either side when Adèle indicated left and turned into a pleasant driveway. At the head of it was a large stone-built house.

'Here we are—the Grange,' Adèle said, bringing the car to a decorous halt on the gravel sweep before the front door. 'Come along, Kate, and I'll introduce you to Maria.'

Because of shift changes and the various vicissitudes of working on the children's ward, it was two days before Kate managed to buttonhole Nell, and then they only had time for the briefest of exchanges before they both had to hurry about their business. Pantomime Ward, which had been quiet when Kate had started her job,

was suddenly full, and not just with tonsilec-
tomies and hernias and short-stay patients,
either. With the coming of the school holidays it
seemed as though every possible ailment had
struck the young of Colney Bay, and Kate was
hard at it from the moment she started in the
morning until she left off at night.

'Nell! I've seen the flat. . .want to talk?'

'Rather, if that means there's room for two.
Canteen, half-twelve?'

'Lovely,' Kate said. The two of them had met
on the stairs, Nell with her arms full of clean
linen—an emergency admission—and Kate
with a black bin-bag bulging with dirty painting
overalls. Nell raised her eyebrows at the bag.

'Why isn't the play-leader carting that lot
around?'

Kate groaned. 'She's only in three days a
week, thanks to all the cuts,' she said bitterly.
'Anyone with a moment to spare helps out, and
sometimes even when they haven't a moment
to spare, either.'

'See you at half-twelve, then. Whoever gets
there first bags a window-table and two salads,
or aren't you dieting?'

Kate laughed. With the advent of summer
almost everyone at the hospital was dieting. It
was so galling to see the beaches crowded with
slender young things when you rushed down
for a quick swim in the evening, especially if
you had bulges.

'Of course I'm dieting; I could do with losing at least five pounds. Right, see you later, then.'

Kate delivered her tray to the playroom and then returned to the ward. Hurrying along to make up a bed in room three, she decided to try to be down in the canteen first—then she could get them both chicken salad, which was popular now that the weather was so hot and frequently disappeared before all the staff had been fed. But as it was she nearly forgot about her meeting altogether.

It was one of those mornings. The new admission was diagnosed by Bob Nettall as a possible Still's disease and Kate, gently getting the flushed and moaning child into bed, was fairly sure that he was right. Little Angela was pale but for two hectic pink spots on her cheeks, and she wept when she was touched and complained of pains all over, but particularly in her knees. A quick examination showed the knees to be swollen, the skin very white and shiny.

'Mr Patrick's coming,' Bob said, while Kate bustled round, getting a bed-cradle so that the weight of the blankets would not make Angela's painful knees worse, and telling Jane, the student, to fetch pads of warmed cotton-wool and some sandbags to support the small knees, for Angela was barely five, and despite the pain she was in she kept thanking Kate for everything she did in a small, exhausted voice.

'Good. He'll be able to prescribe something. Poor little love, she is in a bad way.'

'I've done my best,' Bob said. 'But I'll be happier when Charles has had a look at her. I don't think we've had a Still's disease in before, not since I've been registrar, anyway.'

'I've nursed it a couple of times, and it's always very distressing,' Kate murmured. 'As you can see, as soon as I set eyes on her I put her in a cubicle. . .can't risk one of the other kids knocking into the bed or jarring her. I did mean to ask Sister, but she wasn't in her office, so I took it on myself.'

'Is it usual?' Bob asked. They were outside the cubicle now, leaning against the wall, with Kate watching their small patient through the windowpanes in the door. 'I know Charles is against putting the children in cubicles unless they've a parent with them.'

'I'm sure he'll agree in this case,' Kate said. 'Still's disease isn't something you can play around with. Ah, here comes Sandra; I'll just explain and then I really must go—I've got to sort out the babies before I go to lunch.'

Sandra was briefed on the new admission and went back into the cubicle with Dr Nettall; Kate rushed back to room one, where she had a number of babies awaiting attention—a poor thriver, a six-month-old boy with a severe otitis media, a four-month-old girl with a hiatus hernia and a suspected intestinal obstruction. It looked as though she would have to miss her lunch-break, but fate stepped in in the shape of Sister.

'Kate, you shouldn't still be here,' Adèle said reproachfully, entering room one and going straight to the cubicle where Kate was instructing a sweet-faced cadet nurse, Marilyn, in the careful feeding of the tiny, under-nourished poor thriver. 'Off you go and get something to eat; I'll manage here. . .do me good—give me a chance to see how Marilyn's getting on.'

Marilyn looked terrified at the suggestion, but Kate smiled gratefully at Adèle.

'Sister, you're marvellous,' she said, heading for the door. 'I wouldn't mind missing my lunch-break in the normal way, but today I'm supposed to be meeting Nell to talk about the flat.'

'Then you run along,' Sister said soothingly. 'Now, Marilyn, go along to the kitchen and find the feeds. . .they've all been made up ready. . .and fetch baby Ginette's.'

Kate hurried off with the nice feeling that she couldn't have left her charges in safer hands. She was almost at the canteen before she remembered that she had not mentioned the new admission to Sister, and nearly turned back, but at that moment Nell hailed her.

'At last, Kate! Where on earth have you been? Come on, I managed to bag two chicken salads, a window-table, and two double fruit juices. Now shoot!'

Kate sank into the offered chair and pulled her glass towards her.

'Orange juice—bliss,' she sighed. 'Sorry I'm late; it's been a terribly hectic morning. Now, about the flat. . .'

It was quite a long story, and as she told it Kate relived the whole experience. She had been introduced to Maria, a beautiful dark-haired girl in her late twenties, and to the children, four-year-old Sasha and two-year-old Luciana. They had been charming, and had taken her round the garden flat, which was equally charming, even showing her the garden she would be expected to keep tidy.

'As you can see, it's been let go,' Maria had said apologetically. 'I'm afraid my last tenants were a bad lot, as you can probably tell.'

'In what way were they a bad lot?' Nell asked curiously now through a mouthful of chicken salad. 'Is the place a mess? We could cope with that, I suppose.'

'A mess? Well, the garden's dreadful, the bit that goes with the flat,' Kate admitted. 'But no, it's a bit more complicated than that, and I'll quite understand, Nell, if you want to back out.'

'I can't back out until I know what's wrong with the place,' Nell pointed out righteously. 'Do spill the beans, Kate; don't keep me in suspense.'

'Right. The last people did a moonlight.'

'A what? Oh, you mean they ran off without paying their rent. Hard luck on Maria, but it won't affect us, surely?'

'They left something behind,' Kate said pensively. 'And if we want the flat we'll have to take it with all faults, as they say in the horse-world.'

'What faults?' hissed Nell piercingly. 'Don't be so irritating, Kate. Did you like the place? The set-up? Then tell, for Pete's sake!'

'It's a very pleasant flat, the garden could be delightful, and Maria is just about the best landlady you could imagine,' Kate said provocatively. 'But. . .how do you like livestock?'

'Do you mean there are rats and fleas and things?' Nell said after a short pause. 'Oh, God, not rats and fleas!'

'Dogs,' Kate admitted. 'Two very large red setters called Bonnie and Clyde, believe it or not. And Maria loves those dogs and won't have them turned out or kennelled or anything, but she doesn't want them in her part of the house with two small children, either. So it's have the flat and the dogs, or go without the flat, I'm afraid. And, quite frankly, Nell, I'm so keen to have the flat that I'd take it complete with a dozen dogs rather than lose it. But I realise you may feel very differently.'

'I like dogs all right, but what about the responsibility?' Nell groaned. 'It's bad enough having to exercise one small dog, but two! And red setters at that! Most red setters are mentally retarded, I believe.'

'They are generally scatty,' Kate admitted. 'But I'm willing to have a go. Only not alone, I'm afraid. If you don't want to share then I'll stay in the nurses' home, because it isn't just the dogs—the garden really is large, more than one person could possibly manage. But with the two of us sharing the rent we could easily afford to pay for some help in the garden. Only the dogs would be ours. . .at least, until the owners turn up, if they ever do.'

'Vet's bills,' Nell groaned. 'Dog-food, leads, injections. . .how old are these animals, anyway?'

'Oh, two or three,' Kate said airily, hoping she was not too far out. 'Mature, anyway. They've had all their jabs and so on, so we don't have to worry about that. And the flat's really large. If we wanted we could share four instead of just two.'

'Four! Just how big is it, then?' Nell finished her chicken salad and looked pensively at her empty plate. 'I wonder if apple pudding's on today?' She sighed and slapped her own wrist half-heartedly. 'Now, Eleanor Franklyn, you know very well you're going to lose some weight before your hols!'

'It's got two big double bedrooms, a really lovely sitting-room which overlooks the garden, and what they call all the usual offices, which means a neat little bathroom and loo and a smashing kitchen. The dogs have a part of the old stables, so they don't have to actually live indoors, but Maria, who is soft as a brush, likes them to sleep in the house. On thinking it over, actually, I can't say I blame her. It's a big house, the neighbours are out of shouting distance, I imagine, and dogs are a great deterrent to burglars.'

'I must say it sounds wonderful,' Nell said. 'Look, are you free on Saturday? Shall we go over and clinch things with Maria then? Goodness, we could move in on Sunday if she's agreeable. What is the rent, by the way?'

Kate named a sum which brought a big smile to Nell's face.

'That's marvellous—I can afford that easily.'

'That's split between us,' Kate told her, and saw, with real surprise, that it was possible for Nell's smile to grow even wider. 'So if you want to ask anyone else to share as well we could probably afford all sorts of extras.'

'You found it, Kate, or at least you were offered it first. Do you want anyone else to share?'

'No, not really. I think the two of us will be able to manage the rent, the garden and the dogs without any trouble, and we're in the same wing of the hospital, which will help, too. But you've been here much longer than I have; if you've a particular friend you want to ask along. . .'

'I've been working at the Liz for exactly six weeks,' Nell said, smiling across at Kate. 'Everyone's very friendly, but when I saw your funny little face I thought, hooray, someone newer than me, who looks fun—perhaps a friend. So don't kid yourself that it was you who needed me—it was mutual.'

'What about your boyfriend?' Kate asked curiously. 'When you mentioned your boyfriend I naturally assumed you'd been here ages.'

'No, that's not the case at all. I came here to work near Richard, and then discovered that it wasn't quite as much fun as I thought it would be—he got possessive, bossy. . .we're clearly better with a hundred miles between us. Which means, of course, that I'm doubly in need of a friend and a flat-share.'

'Right. Then we'll meet outside the nurses' home on Saturday morning and see what local transport is like, shall we? If it's bad I'm getting a small motorbike, because, though, of course, I want to learn to drive, Rome wasn't built in a day and I need to be able to get into the hospital at a moment's notice, particularly after Sister leaves. . .always assuming nothing goes wrong, of course.'

'What could stop you?' Nell said cheerfully, getting up and piling the used crockery and cutlery on a tray. 'Back to the grind!'

* * *

Back on the ward once more, Kate walked straight into drama. Directly outside the cubicle with little Angela in it Mr Patrick and young Marilyn were engaged in what looked like an acrimonious discussion, or rather Marilyn, pink-faced and on the verge of tears, was listening to Mr Patrick, trying now and again to get a word in edgeways and failing dismally. Hovering near by, looking unbelievably smug, was Dr Carruthers.

Kate, with more than a suspicion as to what was afoot, hurried over to them.

'Umm. . .excuse me, Mr Patrick, can I. . .?'

Mr Patrick swung round. His brows rose.

'Ah, Staff. I was just telling this young lady. . .' he indicated the embarrassed Marilyn '. . .that the staff nurse on duty had no right to put this case into a cubicle without consulting Sister. As you know, we've only a few such facilities and in general it's better for a child to be nursed on the main ward. . .'

He got no further.

'In general I'd agree with you,' Kate said smoothly. 'But since Angela has Still's disease——'

'Ah! but who diagnosed Still's?'

'Both Dr Nettall and I were of the opinion——' Kate started, and was interrupted.

'Oh, Dr Nettall did the admission, I see. When Dr Carruthers pointed it out to me she was under the impression that the nursing staff had taken it upon themselves to put the child in a cubicle pending diagnosis. So Sister, presumably, put the child in here?'

'Well, no, it was me,' Kate admitted. 'But I've nursed a number of Still's patients before, sir, and because of the pain caused in the inflamed joints it's usually considered unwise to nurse such patients on a general children's ward, where they're liable to be knocked against. So, since I was here and Sister wasn't, I put Angela where you see her.'

'I see.' Mr Patrick glanced down at her. The frown had lifted but he was still not looking too pleased. 'Well, you did right in this instance, Staff. All these arthritis-related diseases need quiet in the early stages. However, Dr Carruthers was certainly right to tell me, since either Sister or I should be the one to decide who goes into the cubicles.' He pushed the door of the cubicle ajar and stepped inside, holding it open so that she could follow him, and Kate, in her turn, held it—though reluctantly—for the houseman. 'Another time bear that in mind, would you? You aren't sister of the ward yet!'

It was said with just enough coolness for Kate to know that it was a reproof, and to simmer crossly. But then he turned to Dr Carruthers.

'All right, Estelle, Staff and I can manage in here now. You can continue with your admission details.'

To Kate's joy the beautiful houseman's ivory pallor turned pink, though she gave no other sign that she had registered her boss's mild disapproval.

'Of course, Mr Patrick,' Dr Carruthers said, leaving the cubicle and shutting the door rather too sharply behind her, so that the child in the bed jumped and moaned, causing Kate to hurry over to her to place a calming hand on the hot forehead.

'It's all right, Angela,' she murmured. 'Sleep now, darling, sleep now.'

Angela sighed but did not wake, so Kate turned back to the surgeon.

'Have you prescribed anything yet, sir?' she asked. 'I monitored the patient's vital signs before I went down for lunch, and the girls have been keeping an eye on her. Her mother should be here soon.'

'I'll prescribe salicylates; you can administer them when they've been dispensed,' Mr Patrick said. 'I see you used a cradle. . .what about her legs? It's affecting her knees, I take it?'

'Yes, that's right. I've put sandbags behind her knees. . .I'll just check them and take her temperature while you examine her.'

Working quickly, the two of them managed the entire examination without once causing the patient to wake, and Kate felt justifiably pleased as the surgeon at last turned away from the bed.

'She'll do,' Mr Patrick said briefly. 'Stay with her in case she wakes until another nurse becomes available. Why didn't her mother come in with her?'

'They sent her in from playgroup,' Kate explained. 'Her mother works in the mornings.'

'I see. Well, you seem to have done a good job with her, Staff. But don't forget—you aren't sister of Pantomime Ward yet.'

He had to have the last word, Kate thought, sitting down quietly in the chair beside the bed. Typical!

Later in the afternoon Mrs Evans, Angela's mother, arrived, tearful and shocked. She saw Angela and, though she wept afresh at the sight of her little daughter's pale face and the cradle keeping the blankets clear of her legs, she was sensible enough to sit down in Sister's office and hear all about the disease which Angela had contracted.

'It's a type of rheumatoid arthritis,' Kate explained carefully, while Sister sat and listened. 'Your daughter is fortunate in that her condition was spotted so quickly by the play-leader, although she thought Angela had acute rheumatic fever, but even so she rushed her in to us in good time. As it is, with careful treatment, lots of bed-rest, splints to keep her limbs straight if they show signs of deformity, and pain-killing drugs, Angela stands every chance of making a full recovery.'

Out of the corner of her eye Kate could see Sister nodding approval.

'That's marvellous,' Mrs Evans murmured thankfully. 'And will she be in hospital long?'

'Still's disease is quite rare, Mrs Evans,' Sister broke in, realising that Kate could not possibly forecast the length of stay which would be necessary. 'But, with good nursing and the right treatment, we'll do our best to make her stay as short as possible. And now would you like to sit with Angela for a bit? She'll probably be waking in a little while and you are the first person she'll ask for.'

Mrs Evans and Sister left the office and Kate followed them out, but then went along the corridor to ward one, where she found Emma Foulds, another staff nurse, changing dressings. Kate joined her and for a while they worked in companionable silence, but when all the dressings were done and the two girls free to talk Kate told Emma about Mr Patrick's condemnation of her putting Angela in a cubicle.

'So if you ask me it was Dr Carruthers trying to get someone into trouble,' she finished bitterly. 'As if I'd do an emergency admission without a doctor, or Sister, or someone!'

'Oh, that's Estelle all over,' Emma said cheerily. 'She'll have a grudge against you, of course.'

'Why ever?'

'Hasn't anyone told you? Estelle's got a sister, Venetia, who's a staff nurse on Geriatrics. She applied for the job here but Adèle wouldn't hear of it, so of course Estelle was pretty cross. And they say Mr Patrick wasn't too pleased either, having more or less promised Estelle that her sister could have the job.'

'Oh, heavens,' Kate said, dismayed. 'Then Mr Patrick can't be feeling too fond of me, either.'

'Mr Patrick's going to find out all about Estelle one of these days, and then he'll be grateful he didn't land himself with Venetia,' Emma said cheerfully, pouring fruit juice. 'The trouble is she's beautiful, and awfully clever at shifting the blame. But her sins will find her out, you'll see.'

Later, on the main ward, Kate surveyed her small charges with satisfaction. They had had their lunch and now they were having their rest, some already placidly slumbering, mouths open, eyes shut. But at the far end of the room, all strung up like a Christmas turkey and with a face which would have done credit to one for redness and bad temper, Suzy glared at the small portable-television screen at the foot of her bed, whose sound had been turned right off, and, when Kate went over and greeted her in a whisper, glared at her as well.

'I'm absolutely fed up,' she said, deliberately keeping her voice to a slightly above-normal pitch. 'You don't know how awful it is to be me, Kate!'

'I can guess, you poor prisoner,' Kate sighed.

'Suzy, why don't I ever come in and see you reading? Or knitting? Or doing jigsaws?'

Suzy shrugged. To Kate's distress she saw the child's chin was quivering.

'Dunno. Readin's school, really, isn't it? And I make an awful mess of knitting; always have done. Jigsaws. . .oh, I dunno.'

'But you like stories,' Kate said, remembering Suzy's fascination whenever *Jackanory* came on the television. Thinking back, she realised that if a visitor read to a little one Suzy would usually try to entice the reader near enough so that she, too, could share the treat. 'Why not just try one of the books from the library? Not the stuff you get here, in the playroom, but something for your age-group. An adventure story. . .' She laughed. 'You could even try the teenage books; they're a bit old, perhaps, but. . .'

Suzy shook her head.

'Nah, I don't fancy reading. I'm. . .I'm not very good, see; it's hard work. Makes me eyes ache, same's too much telly does.' She sighed deeply. 'Wish someone would come and read to me every afternoon. Just quiet, like.'

'I wish one of us had the time. . .' Kate was beginning, when she was struck by inspiration. 'Hang on, Suzy, I've had an idea. Have you ever thought about talking books?'

'What's them?' Suzy asked suspiciously, answering Kate's question.

'They're tapes,' Kate explained. 'They're stories and plays and things, which you can just listen to whenever you feel like it. I'm pretty sure you can borrow them from a local library, which means I could bring some in with me tomorrow if you'd like it.'

'Well, I would,' Suzy said, her face showing more animation than Kate had ever seen on it before. 'That's a good idea, Kate. . . Do them things have earphones, so I could listen quiet, like, while the littl'uns sleep?'

'Oh, bound to have,' Kate said airily, hoping she was right. 'Then I'll fetch some in with me tomorrow morning, and, for today, how about if I fetch you a jigsaw to keep you from going mad with boredom?'

'Sure,' Suzy said, smiling at Kate with real affection. 'Gee, talking books, eh?'

CHAPTER THREE

DESPITE her hopes, when Kate awoke on moving day it was raining. Not hard, but with that light, persistent drizzle which so often seemed to start when you went to the seaside and continued, gently but inexorably, all day.

Kate got out of bed and padded to the window. Next door, in one of the shared rooms, a student nurse with a raucous laugh giggled over something someone had said. Kate glanced at her wrist-watch: only half-past seven; she needed not get up this morning until nine at the earliest. It was only habit which had woken her betimes.

She crossed the room, intending to get back into bed, then shook her head at herself and went to plug her electric kettle in. There was a kitchen just down the corridor, but, like most of the nurses, Kate preferred to make her early-morning tea in her room.

While the kettle was singing she brushed her hair, fished out her sponge-bag from on top of her suitcase, took her dressing-gown from its hook on the door and put it on, and then, as the tea brewed, she padded along to the bathroom.

Nell was coming out of her door as she passed

46

it, clearly intent on the same errand. The two girls stopped, and smiled guiltily.

'Couldn't sleep? Nor me,' Nell admitted. 'Want to come down to the canteen for some grub, or shall we make our own?'

'Let's just have tea and toast in the kitchen,' Kate said quickly. She felt she could not have borne queueing with a crowd of girls and having to wait for her food, not today. Instead she rushed back to her room as soon as she had finished in the bathroom, dressed, and then made for the kitchen.

Nell was there before her, with bread already in the toaster and a tub of low-calorie spread standing by.

'Let's get outside this lot fast,' she begged, already crunching toast. 'And then we can go and get our stuff into the van.'

Nell's boyfriend Richard might have had his faults, but he had raised no demur when invited to help them cart their belongings over to the new flat. Kate rather liked him, in fact, and thought he and Nell could do a lot worse than marry, but she also saw Nell's point about not simply settling for someone until one was sure.

So now they gobbled toast, drained their mugs of tea, and then hurried along to their rooms.

'All my worldly goods are in these cases,' Kate said as she and Nell bumped their luggage down the stairs to the small foyer. 'Whatever my faults, you must admit I do travel light.'

She eyed with disfavour the tottering pile of black dustbin bags and ancient carriers which were propped around her friend's two large suitcases.

'You've never had a place of your own before,' Nell said defensively. 'Just wait till you've been in a week or two—you'll be just as bad as me. Worse, probably.'

'I've no intention. . .' Kate began, but just then Richard's white van drew up outside, Richard pipped the horn, and the move, which they had waited for so eagerly, had begun.

The two girls had moved into the flat on a Saturday, and when they awoke on the Sunday it was fine once more, the sun streaming in through the bedroom windows and casting an unflatteringly strong light on the elderly furnishings and fittings of the garden flat.

'But we'll make it beautiful in no time,' Nell said robustly when Kate sighed over the patched and faded curtains. 'I'm going out with Richard today, to thank him for yesterday—he was a sport, wasn't he, Kate?—but you could go into the garden and pick some flowers. That would brighten things up.'

'It's such a glorious day, I might go out myself,' Kate said rather wistfully as she went out to see Nell off. 'After all, there must be some sort of a bus service on Sunday.'

'Course there is,' Nell said, getting into Richard's van. 'We could give you a lift if you like.'

But this Kate declined, knowing full well that someone would have to take Bonnie and Clyde for a walk and really quite looking forward to a quiet day, tackling the overgrown garden.

But first she must wash up the breakfast things and tidy the kitchen. Getting down to it, she realised ruefully that Nell, delightful though she was, was the sort of flat-mate who would have to be told to do her share. Already she had shown a tendency to take a bath whenever a meal was over. And we've only been in residence twenty-four hours—less, Kate reminded herself. Never mind, they would learn to pull together, and Nell was so good-natured that it wouldn't be long before she did her share as a matter of course. The dogs hung about the kitchen, waiting for her to finish—almost sighing audibly, Kate thought with a smile as they jostled to get near her. But when she opened the back door they rushed out happily enough, racing round the overgrown orchard, disappearing into the shrubbery and finally coming out and casting hopeful glances at the garden gate.

Clearly they were in the habit of taking their walk before getting down to the main business of the day, whatever that was.

Maria must be a late riser on a Sunday, Kate

told herself, going indoors again and clipping on the dogs' stout leather leads. Bonnie and Clyde, obviously used to the procedure, stood still for about three seconds and then tried to leave the garden in different directions, Bonnie heaving her to the right, Clyde to the left. She was almost on her knees, her voice reaching soprano-like heights, when a large hand took both leads from her grasp and a voice said cheerfully, 'What's all this? Get your husband to take one of the dogs—you can't possibly. . .'

'Thanks, but what makes you think. . .? Oh!'

She had thought the voice vaguely familiar, but the face could never have been mistaken for anyone else's. Mr Charles Patrick, her boss, stood above her, smiling down on her without a hint of recognition.

'Umm. . .thanks very much; if you'd just hold them for a moment, until I can persuade them to go in the same direction. . .' Kate began. 'They don't know me very well and I don't know them either.' Wildly she grabbed for the leads again, keeping her face turned away from him so that her soft fawny-gold hair hid her features. That was it, of course. On the ward she had her hair pulled back, uniform, and no make-up. Today she had her hair loose, she was wearing jeans and a close-fitting white T-shirt, and her lashes were darkened and her brows defined with a light brown pencil. But it rather proved that mighty surgeons did not take a lot of notice of inferior people like the nurses on their wards!

It seemed she had wronged him, however. He let her take one lead, but kept a firm hold on the other.

'Oh, it's you, Staff. Visiting Maria? Or may I call you Kate? Look, I was just about to get some exercise—suppose I walk along with you, keep hold of the big chap? We could take them up to the Gorse—it's not very far.'

Kate felt her cheeks begin to burn. How did you tell your boss that this would not be paradise, but purgatory? It was bad enough on the ward, wondering whether he would ever forget seeing her flat on her face like a landed fish, very probably with her knickers showing. How on earth would she manage to act naturally while they walked to the Gorse—wherever that might be? She opened her mouth to find an excuse and heard her voice saying, 'Thanks, that would be marvellous; I'm afraid Clyde—that's the dog—is a good deal too strong for me, but I dare not let him off the lead until we know each other better. Lead on, then, sir.'

'Sir? Very formal for a Sunday morning, aren't we? How old do you think I am?'

Kate bit back the involuntary words—'about two hundred?'—which had risen to her lips and turned to give him an appraising stare. In jeans and a T-shirt not very dissimilar to her own, he, too, she saw, had lost a few of the years she had given him that first day on the ward.

'Hmm. . .mid-thirties?' Kate hazarded, thinking she was being kind.

'Not bad. Thirty-four could be described that way, I suppose. And you'll be. . .?'

'Exactly ten years younger; I'm twenty-four,' Kate admitted. They were walking along now, side by side, and moving fast, two long-legged people who enjoyed exercise. 'You can call me Kate, of course, but I think I'd better stick to Mr Patrick.'

'You'll call me Charles, as Maria does,' the surgeon said cheerfully. 'After all, if I'm going to exercise your dogs for you. . .Now tell me, how come they're suddenly your dogs? A couple of months ago they belonged to a feckless young Irish couple with lots of blarney and very little else. Now what were their names?' He chuckled. 'Probably Mick and Pat, the Pat being short for Patricia, of course.'

'How well did you know them? Not all that well, or you'd have known their names, presumably,' Kate said rather breathlessly. The fast pace suited her, but it didn't leave her with much breath left over for light conversation. 'How did you come to meet them?'

Mr Patrick shrugged. 'I never really did know them—not to speak to,' he confessed. 'Apart from shouting the odd remark like "good morning", I mean. I wouldn't call myself an exercise freak or anything like that, but I do enjoy walking and hill-climbing, so I used to see them out with the dogs now and then. How on earth could they have left the beasts behind?' he added. 'They're probably worth quite a bit of money as well, dogs like these.'

'They're certainly very handsome,' Kate agreed. She had only fed them once—last night—but could well imagine someone balking at the thought of feeding them for long. Clyde ate like a starving tiger and Bonnie wasn't much better, for all that she was smaller and lighter. It was no use telling herself that they had been going short, either, because it was plain that Maria had been filling them up with massive meals. The only thing she had drawn the line at was exercise. . .which was why, Kate supposed sourly, she herself was being towed along at a smart trot towards the not-so-distant hills.

'Here we are,' Mr Patrick said as the road, which had become little more than a track, finally forsook all claim to pavements or tarmac and petered out into a dusty lane leading over a wild and beautiful tract of hilly country with trees, bushes and the inevitable gorse growing everywhere. 'Well, Kate, what do you think of the Gorse?'

Kate looked around her, then breathed deeply. The fresh early-morning air was like wine, the breeze lifted her hair from her over-heated brow, and the sunshine fell like a benison upon her.

'It's marvellous,' she said. 'We'll come here

often, the dogs and I. Do you suppose we might let them off their leads now?'

'Let's take a chance,' Mr Patrick said, suiting action to words. Clyde, with no more ado, set out, tail and ears streaming, for the top of the nearest rise, and Bonnie followed, giving the sort of high, excited yaps that puppies emitted when they saw a rabbit. 'Tell you what, shall I give an experimental holler and see if they come back?'

'Yes, please,' Kate said, seeing, with some dismay, the two wine-coloured dogs disappearing over the ridge. 'I'd never forgive myself if they got run over or something.'

'Run over? Here?' Mr Patrick laughed, then put two fingers into his mouth, emitting the most awful screech and following this up with a stentorian shout of, 'Clyde! Bonnie! Here, fellers!'

When there was no sign of the dogs returning Kate thought that Mr Patrick was about to get his come-uppance and prepared to commiserate with him, and was in fact opening her mouth to do so when over the ridge and charging down towards them came the two dogs, eyes beaming, ears flapping, mouths set in foolish smiles. It was clear that, whatever their faults, they had been well-taught by someone.

'There you are,' Mr Patrick said, walking up the hill now, ahead of the dogs. 'You don't have to worry about them, Kate; they've been well trained. Come on, let's get to the top of the hill—or are you whacked?'

'I'm fine,' Kate said, following him. Together they reached the ridge and stared out across the rolling hills which gradually became mountains, blue with distance. 'I say, what a view!'

'Mm-hmm; the country round here is beautiful,' Mr Patrick agreed. He was standing beside Kate now, so close that she could feel the warmth of him against her shoulder. It gave her a very odd feeling and she moved a little away, but Mr Patrick was having none of it.

'See that mountain there. . .in line with the silver birches? There's a marvellous walk; I do it two or three times each summer. You and the dogs should come with me some time—we could take a picnic, make a day of it. Do you like hill-walking?'

'I've not done any,' Kate said, trying to move unobtrusively away from him again, but he laid a casual hand on her shoulder, pulling her round so that their heads were close together.

'No? Well, the easiest walk for beginners is this side of the mountain. . .can you see that thin white line just above the birches?'

Kate squinted up her eyes and thought she could just make out a fine white thread on the blue-green of the distant hill, but she found herself confused by Charles Patrick's nearness, by the warmth of the hand on her shoulder, the strength of the arm which pulled her close—far too close! She could smell his skin and hair, his aftershave, feel the smoothness of his shirt against her bare arm and found that she was even conscious of the timbre of his voice as he spoke, feeling it echoing through her body as its deep tones echoed around the hillside.

This was absurd!

'Yes, I can see the white line,' Kate said in her most repressive tone. She pointed. 'There! Is that it?'

She thought he would let her go—hoped he would—but instead he just nodded, loosening his hold, to be sure, but still keeping her in the curve of his arm, still with his hand grasping her shoulder. Kate tried to ignore the fact that his touch sent the oddest tingles down her spine and told herself, fiercely, to concentrate on the view and stop being such an idiot.

'Yes, you've got it. It's a stream, in fact, a mountain stream, but, although it has made its own deep gorge over the years, it's still one of the best and easiest ways to get up that particular mountain. Well, Kate? How about coming with me next weekend for the day? Do you good, get your mind off the ward and the patients, give you a complete break.'

It would have been easy enough to say yes now, and then pretend, later, that another unavoidable appointment had come up, but Kate was a forthright girl. Firmly she shook her head, moving away from Mr Patrick as she did so.

'No, Mr Patrick, I don't think that's a very good idea. I mean, I might love hill-walking and I might be quite good at it, but suppose I'm not? Suppose I ruin your day and, to be blunt, you ruin mine? We've got to work together afterwards.'

Mr Patrick looked at her, a dark brow shooting up towards his hairline. He really was good-looking, Kate discovered belatedly, quite the best-looking medic she had ever worked with. But he was first and foremost a surgeon and her boss, not a man with whom she could socialise at all in the usual sense of the word, and she was very sure that trying to pretend they could be friends as well as colleagues would only end in tears.

'Kate, you're being absurd! Do you think me so petty, so small-minded, that I'd hold it against you if you didn't like hill-walking after all? Of course I wouldn't! And, if you're thinking that just because I'm a paediatric surgeon and you're a paediatric nurse we can't possibly share any sort of social life, you're well and truly mistaken! Why, Estelle Carruthers and I have dinner together from time to time, I've been out with Adèle in a foursome. . .get up to date, girl—this is the nineteenth-nineties, not the eighteen-nineties! A man and woman can have á relationship quite other than a romantic one, you know.'

'Oh, yes, I'm sure,' Kate agreed. 'But it would put us on a different footing at work, wouldn't it? I think I prefer to keep my social life and work apart.'

'Well, in this case, I don't,' Mr Patrick said firmly. 'If you don't fancy hill-walking how about sailing? Ever done any? Swimming? Do you drive a fast car? Go shopping in town? Because you might easily bump into me doing any of those things, and what will you do—turn round and walk out of the shop, or leap from the car, or——?'

'All right, I'll come hill-walking,' Kate said, laughing. 'Just don't blame me if you get furious with me and feel you can't bawl me out the way you'd like to!'

Charles Patrick threw back his head and roared with laughter, then shouted for the dogs and set off down the hill again, a hand steadying Kate's elbow when she stumbled on the uneven ground. Kate told herself firmly to ignore the *frisson* of feeling which shot up her arm and along her spine at his touch.

'Don't worry. If I want to shout or find fault I'll shout and find fault; just because we've enjoyed an outing together that doesn't mean you're immune to my rages! Dogs! Come back here at once—don't get too far ahead.'

The dogs obeyed, and for the best part of an

hour Charles Patrick and Kate strolled across the
Gorse, talking, laughing from time to time,
getting to know one another. Kate found that
her boss liked all outdoor sporting activities,
read quite a lot of non-fiction but didn't have
time for all the fiction that interested him, had
done a lecture tour in the States and another in
France, and lived alone.

'I'll invite you up to my place for a meal some
time. I'm in temporary accommodation at the
moment, since I'm having a house built,' he said
lazily, looking down at her, his lids drooping,
those amazing navy blue eyes very bright
beneath the heavily fringed lids. 'I'm a good
cook and I enjoy it, though I'm afraid I can't
claim to do my own housework—a cleaning
lady does that for me.'

'Lucky you,' Kate said enviously. 'I'm sharing
a flat with another nurse, and I do get the feeling
that it's going to be a battle to get either of us to
clean the place. I hate housework but it has to
be done, so my flat-mate and I share the work—
in theory at least.'

'Perhaps, when you're made up to sister,
you'll be able to afford some help in the house,'
Mr Patrick said seriously. 'I don't see why you
shouldn't. After all, men who aren't married
invariably get someone in to clean.'

'A sister's salary may be better than a staff
nurse's,' Kate said, smiling, 'but I don't imagine

it is quite on a level with the amount a paediatric surgeon takes home each month.'

'Well, possibly not,' Mr Patrick said, looking innocent. 'But it wouldn't cost that much just to have someone in for, say, three hours a week to do the cleaning. Anyway, think about it when you get your upgrading. When do you suppose it will be? Sister goes all coy whenever I ask.'

'She said within two months, or sooner if she thought we could manage without her,' Kate told him. 'I'm used to a children's ward, of course, but every hospital has its pet ways of doing things, so I'll sort them out before I start encouraging Sister to leave.'

'I'm glad you said that because it gives me a chance for a little gentle criticism,' Mr Patrick said. They were walking down the road again with the dogs on their leads but quite content, now that they had had a good run, to walk sedately beside them. 'I've steered clear of shop talk, but there's a point I'd like to make.'

'Fire ahead,' Kate said cheerfully. They had got on so well and he had been so easy that she could not imagine his criticism was likely to be very basic. 'What have I done?'

'Given young Suzy story-tapes.'

'Oh!' Kate said blankly. 'I thought I was being rather bright.'

'Yes, you were. In a way. But you see, Kate, Suzy's a very slow reader. She has a tutor who comes in for a couple of hours each morning, and Miss Gibson—that's the tutor—is keen that Suzy is given every encouragement to read. Apparently she saw the talking books and complained to Dr Carruthers that you were undermining her hard work. Now, as I told Estelle Carruthers, that was the last thing on your mind, but. . .'

They had reached the gate leading to Maria's house. Kate dragged her dog to a halt and reached out, fairly snatching the lead from Mr Patrick. The idea! That Estelle Carruthers should pass on a spiteful bit of gossip about her to Mr Patrick was infuriating enough, but that he should see fit to pass it on to her as a legitimate complaint. . .Well, it made her blood boil!

'I'm sorry that you should see it that way, Mr Patrick,' Kate said, 'but, quite frankly, if that was what Miss Gibson said then she knows nothing about children. One way to make sure that Suzy never enjoys reading is by debarring her from stories and allowing the dreadful boredom of the afternoon rest period to continue. As it is, I'll speak to Miss Gibson myself—Miss Gibson, Mr Patrick, not Dr Carruthers!'

'Don't you think it's a trifle high-handed of you to assume that you know better than Miss Gibson, who has been tutoring children for thirty years?' Mr Patrick said as Kate whisked through the gateway. 'After all, Kate, you're only twenty-four and you've nursed sick children, not taught them. Don't you think, in this instance, that experience should be allowed its say?'

'Possibly. I'll speak to Miss Gibson,' Kate said. This was more of Estelle's work, she was sure! The dogs, seeing their home before them, began to tug dementedly on their leads and her voice came out in jerks. 'But, since the story-tapes were given to Suzy for use in her spare time, I can't imagine any sensible woman objecting.' Kate began to walk up the drive towards the house, calling over her shoulder, 'Goodbye, Mr Patrick; thank you for your help.'

'Perhaps if you could get story-tapes which fitted in with Suzy's reading programme?' Mr Patrick's voice, close to Kate's ear, proved that he had actually had the temerity to follow her instead of simply accepting her tactful dismissal. 'Would you like me to have a word with Dr Carruthers, find out just what Miss Gibson meant when she said you were undermining her work?'

Kate stopped short—not an easy thing to do with the dogs tugging desperately. She turned. Mr Patrick was right at her elbow!

'I'll have a word with Miss Gibson,' she repeated. I must go in now, Mr Patrick. . . Did you come up the drive to visit Maria?'

'I came up the drive because it leads home,' Mr Patrick said placidly. 'Here, you'll never get the door unlocked while those goofy dogs tug like that; let me. . .'

'I'm all right,' Kate said crossly, though she had little choice but to allow him to take the leads from her. She unlocked her door, then did a double take, her eyes rounding with shock. 'It leads home?'

'That's right. I've got the flat directly above you,' Mr Patrick said cordially; Kate could almost hear the suppressed amusement in his voice. 'Didn't Maria tell you? Dear me—well, it's a pleasant surprise for you, really, I dare say, since if the buses aren't convenient you'll be able to beg a lift.' Kate continued to stare and he put out a hand and chucked her under the chin in a manner she afterwards decided was thoroughly offensive. 'Goodbye for now, Kate! Don't forget our hill-walking expedition next Sunday!'

'He's in the flat above, I tell you!' Kate's voice rose to an uninhibited squeak. 'Nell, if I'd known. . .well, I never would have moved in. Whatever was Sister thinking of?'

'Matchmaking again,' Nell said with a chuckle. The two girls had just eaten a meal and were washing and drying up after it, Kate at the sink and Nell wielding the tea-towel. 'I did warn you what Adèle was like once she'd got the bit between her teeth.'

'I must say, it does seem a bit odd that she said the top flat was unoccupied,' Kate confessed. 'Thinking it over, I can see that she might have kept the information to herself about Mr Patrick and hoped that we'd not mind, or not notice him or something. But to say there was no one in the flat. . .'

'Ask her tomorrow,' Nell advised. 'But personally, joking apart, I don't think she would have deceived you deliberately.' She finished drying the plates and put them back on the old-fashioned dresser. 'Is that it, then? Shall we take some coffee through into the living-room and watch telly?'

'No reason why not,' Kate said, taking off the rubber gloves and lying them tidily on the draining-board. 'I could do with a nice sit-down. I didn't tell you what I did after walking the dogs, did I?'

'Nope,' Nell said, pouring coffee. 'Surprise me!'

'I started on the garden and got so involved that I didn't leave off until stiffness and thirst drove me indoors,' Kate confessed. 'The dogs helped, and had to be driven off the rose-beds with shouts and yells, but I got a tremendous lot done—it looks much better. You can take a squint in the morning when it's light enough to see properly.'

'I will,' Nell promised, picking up the coffee-cups and heading for the sitting-room. 'You mean you were out there, weeding and so on, knowing Mr Patrick might be looking down on you? Literally as well as figuratively, I mean.'

'It's part of our agreement for the flat,' Kate pointed out. 'And, anyway, I thought it over and made a decision. I'm going to pretend that Mr Patrick's simply the tenant of the flat upstairs. But just wait till I see Sister tomorrow!'

'My dear child, I promise you that I had no idea the upstairs tenant was Mr Patrick,' Sister assured Kate as they checked the patients' notes over on the Monday morning. 'If I'd known I'd still have recommended the place to you, but I'd certainly have told you what exalted company you were keeping! When did he move in?'

'I didn't ask. Oh, well, the damage is done now, and we're both so in love with the flat and the dogs and everything that neither Nell nor I would change it for a luxury apartment on the sea-front,' Kate assured the older woman. 'But you can look out for sparks if what Mr Patrick told me about Miss Gibson is true!'

She repeated the story to Sister, who pulled a face.

'Miss Gibson is a sensible woman and Dr Carruthers is a trouble-maker with her eye on any eligible male, and they don't come much more eligible than Charles Patrick,' she declared roundly. 'Have a word with Miss Gibson, Kate, but I'm sure you'll find she made some innocent remark and Estelle deliberately misconstrued it so she could go running to Charles. But don't hold it against him, because he won't be fooled by Dr Carruthers's pretty face for very long.'

Kate agreed to see Miss Gibson, and the opportunity came later that morning when she was preparing one of her small patients for Theatre. She had given the pre-med and was changing the child carefully into a clean theatre gown when the tutor approached. She smiled at Kate but would have gone straight past had not Kate finished her task and jumped to her feet.

'Oh, Miss Gibson, could I have a word?'

'Of course, Staff,' Miss Gibson said comfortably. She was a plump middle-aged woman with greying hair and a pleasant manner, popular with children and staff alike. 'How can I help you?'

Kate swiftly outlined the story of Suzy and the tapes, and Miss Gibson smiled encouragingly.

'Yes, she told me. It was an excellent idea, Staff, and one which I fully intend to steal for some of my other patients! Is there anything else?'

'No, but I rather got the impression you weren't too pleased, because of Suzy's poor reading. In fact, something Dr Carruthers let drop. . .'

'I did mention it to Dr Carruthers,' Miss Gibson said, frowning. 'Now, let me see, exactly what did I say?' Her brow cleared. 'Yes, I remember, I said what a good idea it was,

especially for a child who found reading difficult, and Dr Carruthers said she just hoped it
wouldn't make Suzy lazy.' Miss Gibson
laughed. 'So you see, Staff, how things get
twisted. . . Dear me, I wish everyone took as
much interest in my pupils as you and the other
nurses do!'

Kate made some non-committal reply and
returned to her patient, but she felt that fore-
warned was forearmed. She would treat Dr
Carruthers with great caution in future, and she
could not help hoping that it would not be too
long before Mr Patrick, too, learned not to
believe every word his pretty houseman uttered.

CHAPTER FOUR

'KATE, will you be long? If not I'll order you a salad, shall I?'

Kate, monitoring a new patient's vital signs, pulled a face at her friend but continued to count pulse-beats until she was satisfied, then laid the small boy's arm gently back on the sheet and began to fill in the details on his chart.

'Hello, Nell,' she said absently. 'I'll be about ten minutes, if that's soon enough? Mr Patrick's doing a ward round directly after lunch, so I want to be back in good time.'

'Fine,' Nell said. 'What's up with that little chap? Doesn't he look an angel?'

Kate glanced ruefully down at the small face on the pillow, the light lashes firmly closed, the mouth a little open.

'He's had his tonsils out,' she said. 'But don't let the angelic looks fool you. Before he went down he reduced three nurses to nervous wrecks and I was one of them! Master Elvis Lloyd is going to make us long to be coal-miners or steeplejacks or in some other low-risk profession—in fact, anything bar nurses—before he leaves us.'

'One of those, eh?' Nell chuckled sympathetically. 'Still, you always say you need a naughty patient to keep the rest on their toes.'

'Yes, but there's naughty and downright dreadful, and Elvis comes into the latter category—mind you, with a name like Elvis. . .'

At the sound of his name the small boy stirred, and Kate hastily took his hand in hers, giving Nell a dismissive little wave as her friend set off down the ward once more.

'Elvis? You've had your operation, darling, and you're back on the ward. Kate's here; you're quite all right.'

Elvis groaned and his small hand tightened in Kate's for a moment before his lashes trembled and blue eyes stared foggily up at Kate.

'Oh. . .oh, Katie, my mouf's dry!'

'Yes, it would be, but you can't have a drink just yet, poppet. Would you like a mouthwash?'

Elvis ran a tongue round his dry lips.

'What *is* it?' he demanded suspiciously. 'Does it hurt?'

Kate laughed.

'No, of course not! It's just stuff to wash your mouth. . .' She stopped short, memories of parental threats concerning mouth-washing coming into her mind. 'Look, I'll fetch some.'

But Elvis, when she returned with the mouth-hygiene pack, was sleeping again, so Kate detailed one of the pupil nurses to sit by the bed, ready to use the mouth-wash should the child decide it would help, and, having checked her other patients with a glance, hurried along the corridor and out of the ward. In the canteen Nell and two light lunches awaited her. At a window-table, what was more, so that they could look out on the people hurrying along the promenade and could even envy those lucky enough to be lazing on the beach in the hot sun.

'Marvellous,' Kate said gratefully, sinking into her seat. 'When we've eaten I'm going to rush up to town for a few minutes. In the struggle to get young Elvis off to Theatre my tights were kicked to bits. . .look!' She exhibited a stupendous series of ladders down her right leg. 'He was barefoot too—surprising what a craftily angled toenail can do!'

'I'll come with you,' Nell said promptly. 'Is this the first time you've seen Mr Patrick since not going hill-walking with him?'

'Yes, it is. And I don't mind admitting I'm a trifle apprehensive.'

'I don't see why; you have a right to change your mind.'

'I knew it was a mistake from the start,' Kate admitted gloomily, tucking into a generous cheese salad with a large chunk of crusty French bread. 'I told him it was. . .but at least the fates helped me to get out of it.'

'You mean Sister Archer's absence helped you get out of it,' Nell reminded her with a grin. 'Mind you, I'm sure admin would have come up with an alternative if you hadn't volunteered your services that weekend.'

'Yes, probably. But would it have been someone worthy of being left in charge of Adèle's precious babies for two whole days?' Kate said, twinkling. 'Sister Archer's been doing weekends for ages, but the replacement admin suggested hadn't worked on paediatric before. Anyway, Adèle would have done the extra couple of days herself if I hadn't volunteered, and she needs her rest now.'

'Probably you're right. What was wrong with Archer, anyway?'

'Fortunately it was only a bad cold, so she'll be all right for next weekend,' Kate said, taking a sip of her tea. 'But Adèle agrees that we'll have to have someone standing by who is familiar with the kids; otherwise it over-strains the staff.'

'True. But, once Sister's left, won't she come in if there's an emergency?'

'I don't think she's thought that far ahead,' Kate admitted. She balanced the last of her cheese on the last of her French bread, ate it, and pushed back her chair with a happy sigh. 'Delicious! I'm off now. . .coming?'

'Sure.'

The two girls walked companionably out of the canteen, through the hospital and across the car park to the side-street which would lead them into town. It was a glorious day, and as they walked almost everyone smiled at them, recognising the uniform if not the wearers.

'What did Mr Patrick say when you told him?' Nell asked presently. 'Wish I'd been a fly on the wall! Bet it's the first time in his whole *life* that he's been stood up by a date!'

'Don't be silly! First, it wasn't a date, it was just a walk. Second, I didn't stand him up, I had to cancel as I was working. And third. . .well, third is that he was a bit stiff about it, but he did say "some other time". Only I'll just say no from the start if there is another time,' she added firmly. 'I've realised he's not an easy man to work for.'

'Had more disagreements?' Nell asked.

'No-oo, not really. It's just that we don't always see eye to eye.'

Nell let the matter drop, but, once back on the ward, in her new, unladdered tights, Kate wondered whether the paediatrician would mention that there had been a difference of opinion again between herself and Dr Carruthers when he did the round presently.

The disagreement had been over the lively and terrible Elvis, what was more. Elvis's mother, a thin, ineffectual blonde with a childish, piping voice, had been cuddling him when the call had come for him to go down to Theatre. Kate had advised her to continue cuddling the child as she put him on the trolley, and to accompany him to Theatre so that until he lost consciousness he would be aware of his mother's presence.

Dr Carruthers, however, had taken it upon herself, on meeting the trolley pushed by Kate, to despatch Mrs Lloyd to one of the waiting areas. Elvis, on being deprived of his mother, had fought like a lion with teeth and claws and Kate had had to send for Mrs Lloyd, assuring her that she would be welcome in the ante-room. Dr Carruthers had shot a positively evil look at Kate before marching grimly off down the corridor, clearly intent on telling someone that the new staff nurse had gone too far this time!

But either she had not had the opportunity to tell Dr Patrick or he had not risen to the bait, because when the surgeon and his team arrived on the ward no mention was made of the incident. Kate duly accompanied the round, speaking when spoken to, feeling very much in charge since Sister had taken an afternoon off to go to her ante-natal clinic. Mr Patrick was polite to her—not friendly, as he was with Sister, but perfectly polite, and Kate was beginning to think that the paediatrician was resigned to a normal working relationship with his senior staff nurse when, by Suzy's bed, he suddenly gestured the team to go ahead and dropped behind them to walk beside Kate.

'Well, Staff, I understand you worked the weekend shift last weekend.'

'That's right, sir,' Kate said rather woodenly, regarding the foot of Suzy's bed with fixed attention.

'Good, good. So you'll be taking at least a day off this week, of course?'

'No, sir,' Kate said, surprised into looking up at him. 'There's no need, I won't——'

'Nonsense, Staff! I had a word with Adèle, told her to put you down for a day in lieu. Thursday. So don't show your face in here on Thursday. Right?'

'Th-thank you very much, sir,' Kate stammered. 'But there was really no need——'

'You must let me be the judge of that.'

They caught up with the rest of the team at that point and Mr Patrick said nothing more, though Kate fumed over the high-handedness of the surgeon's action and over his assumption that she was not capable of working twelve days on the trot without a break. But still, a day off would be rather nice, she consoled herself. She would do some shopping, take the dogs out, garden a bit, go for a swim. . .

Missing the bus was always annoying but Kate was used to it, since hospital shifts were never quite what they seemed. On this particular evening, though, it was so warm and bright that she decided she might as well walk. Two miles was a good way but the half-hourly bus service was stretched at this time of evening and she would almost certainly have had to stand all the way home.

She had not gone far, however, when a car drew up beside her. Kate ignored the winding down of the window and the subsequent, 'Hey!' She had no intention of being picked up by a total stranger, and who else was there in Colney Bay but total strangers? But she was wrong.

'Kate! I'm going home—care for a lift?'

'Oh!' Kate felt her cheeks grow warm. Of course, it would have to be Mr Patrick! 'Oh. . .thanks very much. I missed the bus so I thought I'd have to walk, but. . .'

'But you won't,' Mr Patrick concluded cheerfully. He leaned across and opened the passenger-door and Kate sank thankfully down on to the dull red leather seat. 'A bit of luck my spotting you on the pavement because I rather wanted a chat.'

'Oh?' Kate said, full of foreboding. 'About the ward?'

Mr Patrick laughed; he sounded genuinely amused.

'No, indeed. About our mountain walk.'

'Oh!' Kate said again. 'I'm sorry, but——'

'What do you have to be sorry about? I mean our mountain walk this coming Thursday, when we both happen to have a day off.'

Kate compressed her lips.

'I'm busy this Thursday,' she said firmly. 'Very busy.'

'Yes, of course you are. You're fully engaged, in fact. You're walking with me, remember?'

'I'm not. I'm gardening, and exercising the dogs, and——'

'You can exercise the dogs just as well over the mountains as you can on the Gorse,' Mr Patrick said placidly. 'For heaven's sake, Kate, I shan't eat you! What's more, I've booked a table for lunch at a little pub I know; they've agreed we can take the dogs in, too.'

Kate shot him an astonished glance and mumbled something beneath her breath. The surgeon's brows climbed.

'What was that? Don't you *like* being taken out to lunch?'

'I don't like being taken for granted,' Kate said without much thought. 'I don't like having plans made for me without my prior knowledge or consent. I don't like——'

'Hang on, I haven't defended myself against the first two accusations yet. Being taken for granted. . .hmm, makes us sound like an old married couple, Miss Reagan! And, remember, you *did* promise to come hill-walking, only you were unavoidably detained.'

Kate sniffed; he sounded far too sure of himself, far too smug!

'Yes, last Sunday, not next Thursday.'

'The better the day the better the deed,' Mr Patrick said, grinning at her. Kate swallowed. When he looked like that she couldn't help melting towards him, just a little. 'Come on, Kate, be a sport! You'd have come last Sunday if you'd been free—I made a point of seeing that you were free on Thursday so that you could enjoy the treat!'

This time Kate laughed; she couldn't help herself. A treat, was it? Mr Patrick had far too high an opinion of himself! But it was true—she had agreed to have a go, and perhaps it was better to go on her day off and make sure he never asked her out again. . .probably the dogs would do it for her, she reflected, remembering some of the less endearing habits of the two setters.

'Very well, then, since you ask so nicely! What time do we start?'

He patted her knee, then swung the car into their drive.

'I'll call for you at nine, shall I? That will give us a nice long day.'

'It certainly will,' Kate said rather gloomily. 'Wouldn't half-past ten be nicer? I mean, it would let me savour not having to get up a bit more!'

'Well, all right, ten-thirty it is, then,' Mr Patrick agreed. He drew the car to a halt outside the garden flat front door. 'For a first hill-walk perhaps it's as well not to try to go too far.'

He got out of the car, came round and opened the passenger-door. Kate jumped out and heard the dogs begin to bark.

'Maria says they're quiet and good all day,' Kate said over her shoulder, heading for the stable door. 'But they seem to sense when help is at hand and start barking the moment I come into the drive.'

'Do you want a hand?' Mr Patrick said. 'What happens when you open the door?'

'Watch!' Kate invited him mischievously, swinging the door wide.

Bonnie and Clyde erupted from their roomy prison and cast themselves at Kate in between belting round and round the back yard like mad things, occasionally pausing in mid-flight to hurl their leggy bodies briefly up against Mr Patrick's chest. Rather to her annoyance, he stood firm, though she herself staggered beneath the loving onslaught. Clearly he had seen the dogs released before.

She voiced the thought aloud and Mr Patrick grinned.

'Yes, from the safety of my flat,' he said. 'See that window up there? That's my kitchen. I admire the way you hold your own against them, actually.'

'You mean I don't shriek and run,' Kate said. 'I was tempted at first, but I knew it would make things worse.' She went across to her back door and put the key in the lock. 'All right, you two? Coming in now?'

'I'd better go up and get the kettle going too,' Mr Patrick said. 'I'm dying for a cuppa.'

Before she had thought Kate had swung her door wider.

'I'm just going to put the kettle on as well,' she observed. 'Want a cup down here first?'

'Lovely,' Mr Patrick said. He followed her through the doorway and looked curiously round the kitchen. 'This is very pleasant—smaller than my flat, but cosier, too.' He wandered round while Kate assembled cups, teapot and milk, looking at the pictures, the various pans and bottles and tins which were balanced on the shelves. Kate, with a thousand questions to ask, saw an opportunity.

'We'll do a lot to it as time goes on,' she said. 'But we've only been in just about ten days. How about you, Mr Patrick? Have you lived in the top flat for long?'

'Not long,' Mr Patrick said simply. 'Maria offered me the garden flat and two lovely dogs as companions, but I steeled myself against temptation.' He fondled the smooth and silky head of Bonnie, who was pressed against his knees. 'Despite Maria's hopes, I am *not* a soft touch.'

'Meaning I am?' Kate asked suspiciously.

Mr Patrick grinned. 'If the cap fits. . . Ah, tea!'

'Shall we drink it in the living-room?' Kate said. She started to pick up the tray but he was before her, whisking it up and going ahead of her through the kitchen door and into the small living-room with its shabby but pleasant furniture. 'This is rather nice too—are the dogs allowed in?'

'Always have been, judging from the amount of red fur everywhere,' Kate admitted. 'Only not officially on the furniture. . .Clyde, get down!'

'Then why is this chair covered with fur?' Mr Patrick said suspiciously. He was wearing a dark suit with a white shirt, and to sit on that particular chair would mean he would be almost as furry as the dogs, Kate realised. It's awful, but I'd still rather enjoy seeing him discomposed, she realised guiltily. He was far too self-assured and pleased with himself!

'I said they weren't allowed; I didn't say they wouldn't go on the chairs,' Kate pointed out primly. 'Try this one; they don't care for it for some reason.'

She indicated a chair and then sat herself on the couch, which was leather and usually fur-free. Mr Patrick promptly came and sat down beside her. Oh, little Miss Muffet, Kate thought wildly, trying to edge away, I know *just* how you felt when that spider arrived on the scene!

'Milk? Sugar?' Kate leaned forward over the tray, managing to put a little bit more distance between herself and her companion. Ridiculous to feel so self-conscious over a man's nearness, but he had a weird sort of attraction. . .it must be the attraction of terror, she decided, because he really wasn't her type. Vernon Crisp, her most serious boyfriend so far, had been a fair-haired, rosy-cheeked lad, much admired by all the nurses. An ambulance-driver, he had asked Kate out within moments of bringing a patient on to her ward, and the two of them had remained close for some while until Vernon had fallen for the charms of a rosy-cheeked fair-haired girl in Casualty who was so like him to look at that people had taken them for brother and sister. Kate had been a little shocked at how pleased she was for them, how honestly she had been able to say she understood.

She had thought, then, that she was cold. . .well, perhaps I am, she told herself now, demurely pouring tea, but Charles Patrick certainly has the ability to make me feel very warm and involved, far from indifferent. She cast him a quick glance as she passed him his cup and was horrified to realise that she was wondering what it would be like to be kissed by him! Watch yourself, Kate, she warned silently. You're a career nurse, remember, quite happy with other people's babies, not searching for marriage and a family, and this is an experienced man of the world, not an ambulance-driver with a weakness for quiet girls.

'Thank you.' Mr Patrick took the tea and sat back, sipping. Then he talked about hill-walking, what she should wear on Thursday, whether they would go walking if the weather turned wet. He made her laugh, too, and fussed the dogs and played with Clyde's tug-toy, so that when he stood up to leave Kate was conscious of an emotion which was almost disappointment. Nell was going straight out from work tonight; a long, lonely evening loomed ahead.

But Mr Patrick, of course, was unconscious of this. He thanked her for the tea, reminded her again about Thursday, and left, ducking his dark head under her washing-line and raising a hand as he saw her watching him through the window.

Kate went back into the kitchen and began to make the dogs' meal, then went into the pantry and got out the ingredients to make scrambled eggs on toast and a milk pudding. Blow the diet—she was sick of salads! As she worked she was conscious of that warm glow she had thought about earlier. He was a *very* attractive man—there was no doubt about that!

Thursday morning, as luck would have it, dawned fair. Kate, lying luxuriously in bed and sipping the cup of tea Nell had brought her, saw the sunshine flooding through the gap in the curtains with mixed feelings. A sunny day was always nice, but if it had been raining she would have had the perfect excuse for *not* hill-walking. Not that she did not want to hill-walk—that was the ridiculous part. She wanted to go out with

Mr Patrick, was looking forward to it. What she did *not* want was any sort of emotional involvement. She had had a lot of fun with Vernon but she simply hadn't wanted to get serious. And Vernon, in the end, had wanted just that. He had been no more than twelve months older than she, yet he had wanted to settle down, have a home and children. And Kate, a member of the sex which traditionally wanted to settle down with a home and children, found herself not at all keen to lose her independence. Not that you run much risk of it, going out with a paediatrician, she reminded herself. A bit above your touch, Kate Reagan! So just enjoy his company and stop worrying, because he isn't likely to ask you to abandon your career for love!

But that, she knew, was not the worst thing that could happen. The worst thing would be to fall in love with someone who did not return your feelings. So all in all it would be a good deal safer not to get involved.

But all this was pretty silly, really. Kate swung her legs out of bed and hurried into the bathroom, where she showered briskly, put on a loose shirt and a tough pair of jeans, added thick socks and sturdy shoes and set off for the kitchen. She had barely met Mr Patrick—this first date, if you could call it that, was merely for a walk in the hills accompanied by two boisterous dogs—yet here she was, actually worrying about their future! Daft!

He'll probably have a miserable time heaving me along and disciplining the dogs and never ask any of us anywhere again, Kate told herself, munching toast. Just because he's your boss. . .just because he's one of the most attractive men you've met. . .don't start reading too much into it!

It was good advice, but hard to follow. Because Kate, who had always thought of herself as cool, sensible, and not a bit romantic, was suddenly *aware* of Charles Patrick in a way which she had never known before. Steve, Paul, Vernon, Christopher. . .none of them had ever caused her heart to thump quite so loudly, nor her pulses to race.

Perhaps Charles Patrick and I are on the same wavelength, she pondered while the dogs sat and gazed longingly at her toast, following it from plate to mouth, from mouth back to plate, like Wimbledon spectators. Except that Wimbledon spectators, by and large, didn't salivate at the sight of a ball, thought Kate with a smile.

Clyde sighed and shuffled closer and Bonnie, not to be outdone, whined beneath her breath. Giving up, Kate divided the last slice of toast between them, stood up, put her plate and cup in the sink and consulted her wrist-watch. Ten o'clock, and since the weather was determinedly fine she need not worry about cagoules or an extra woolly. But just to be on the safe side she added a thinnish sweater to her clothing, tying it round her waist by its arms. She fiddled with her hair, tying it back, letting it loose, plaiting it, then leaving it loose again, and then a glance at the clock told her that it was only minutes to ten-thirty, so she had better get a move on.

It was the work of seconds to check her outfit, put a rubber band round her hair again to keep it out of the way, get down the dogs' leads and make for the back door. Outside she saw Charles Patrick already backing the car out of the garage and was amused to see the dogs begin to dance with excitement. Plainly they regarded car-rides with great enthusiasm, though to her knowledge they had not ridden in a car for a good few weeks.

'Morning, Kate; nice that you're on time. Hop in.'

Mr Patrick ushered the dogs into the back and then helped Kate—who needed no assistance—into the passenger-seat. The dogs, dancing up and down on the upholstery, pressing large wet noses to the windows and panting a lot, seemed to be encouraging their human companions to get going at once, but first Mr Patrick turned round and wound a couple of inches of window down on his side, and Kate did the same on hers.

'There! Since Mick and Pat neither owned nor drove a car, at least not while they were living at Maria's place, I imagine this drive will have all the excitement of novelty to our furry friends. Perhaps, however, they'll concentrate on what they

can see out of the window and not try to organise
a boarding party to storm the front seats,' Mr
Patrick said hopefully. 'Comfortable, Kate?'

'Very comfortable, thank you. What sort of a
car is this?'

'A Saab turbo.' He patted the steering-wheel
in a clearly spontaneous gesture of affection. 'Do
you like it?'

'It's gorgeous,' Kate admitted. 'It's. . .it's
quite fast, isn't it?'

Her companion chuckled.

'If you think this is fast——'

'No, I'm sure it isn't; I'm sure this is nothing
to what it could do,' Kate said hastily. 'Don't
forget the dogs. . .Bonnie's car-sick at speed.'

The gleaming dark red car, which had begun
to pick up speed in a sinister fashion, suddenly
reduced its pace. Kate, who was not keen on
fast driving, exhaled slowly and turned to give
the two dogs a grateful glance.

'Is she all right?' Mr Patrick asked absently.
'Not far now—only a couple of miles or so.'

Bonnie's long, aquiline nose was well out of
the car window, her nostrils clearly drinking in
the wind of their going. Kate smiled to herself.
The wind had caught the dog's long, fringed
ears and whipped one into an upright position
so that Bonnie resembled a traffic policeman
signalling 'stop!' or, alternatively, a level cross-
ing signalling 'go!'.

'I expect she'll last out if it's only a few miles,'

she said, sincerely hoping that she spoke the truth. But since she had no idea whether a dog could be car-sick, far less whether Bonnie was, she thought it best to change the subject . 'I brought their leads, of course, but shall we be able to let them run free, Mr Patrick? It's more fun for them.'

'Well, they're all right on the Gorse. We'll try it, anyway. And please call me Charles, Kate. After all, we're not in the hospital now.'

'I shall feel silly,' Kate mumbled, 'but I'll try.'

'Good. And, to encourage you, if you slip up and call me Mr Patrick again you'll have to pay a forfeit.' He turned and gave her a wicked little grin. 'How about that for a bribe. . .or do I mean threat?'

'You mean threat,' Kate said faintly. 'What sort of forfeit, M. . . I mean, Charles?'

The surgeon grinned again.

'Aha! Slip up and you'll find out! Here we are, then!'

He turned the car on to a large grassy area, parked and then climbed out and opened the back door.

'I'll put Clyde on his lead while you deal with Bonnie,' he said briskly. 'We'll start off like that, then let them free once we're satisfied that they'll behave themselves.'

'Sure,' Kate said, clipping Bonnie's lead on. 'Off we go!'

CHAPTER FIVE

'RIGHT you are, dogs!' Charles Patrick ushered two exhausted but happy dogs into the back seat and slammed the door on them. 'Well, I never thought to see the day when I tired out those great animals of yours, but I believe they'll sleep like babies all the way home.'

'They won't be the only ones,' Kate admitted, sinking into the passenger-seat and leaning back against the cushioned upholstery. 'What a day!'

'I won't insult you by asking if you enjoyed it because you so plainly did, but are you very tired?'

'Yes, but with a nice, pleasant sort of tiredness,' Kate said. 'What wonderful countryside! I'll never forget the view from the top of the mountain where we had our picnic.'

Because of the glorious weather Charles had decreed that they would picnic instead of going for a pub lunch, and Kate had been happy to comply. In the mountains, with the air like wine and the sunshine so warm, the last thing she had wanted was to have to return to civilisation just to eat. Instead the two of them had shared cold bacon, baps, tomatoes and clear mountain-spring water; not a huge meal, but just right for an energetic day.

'It's been an unforgettable experience,' Charles said softly. 'And it isn't over yet. We're going out for our meal after all, because I could eat a horse!'

'Nowhere smart, I hope,' Kate said drowsily. 'I'm a mess, and I shall probably fall asleep the moment the car starts.'

Charles started the engine and drove forward into the brilliance of the sunset.

'Don't worry, we'll go to a pub which caters for mountain-walkers. And we'll leave the dogs to sleep it off on the back-seat.'

'I don't think they'll stir,' Kate said. 'They must have walked at least five times as far as we did, the way they tore ahead and raced back every couple of minutes.'

'Yes, you've certainly done your duty by them today.' The car nosed on to a stretch of straight, picked up speed, then slackened off as the sharp bends loomed. 'I think we both deserve a steak.'

An hour later, replete, the two of them returned to the car. On the back seat the dogs lay sprawled, but raised their heads and wagged their tails gently as Charles and Kate took their places in the front.

'You shall be fed the moment we get home, and, to help you to last out, here's half a cold bacon bap each,' Kate said, dividing the last of the picnic between the dogs. Bonnie and Clyde sniffed, gulped, and looked hopeful. Charles laughed.

'It'll take more than half a bap to satisfy those appetites! To tell you the truth, I've ever seen a slim girl eat the way you did!'

'It was rather shaming,' Kate admitted. 'I meant to save some of the steak for the dogs, but somehow it just disappeared.'

'Along with a mound of duchesse potatoes, a pile of chips, and three different vegetables,' Charles said approvingly. 'I do hate a girl who plays with her food; you can best be described as a serious eater!'

'Hey, you're no slouch when it comes to putting it away,' Kate protested. 'What about that wonderful summer pudding?'

'What about the cheese and biscuits?'

'At least I didn't have cheese and biscuits,' Kate reminded her companion. 'I thought I might burst after the pudding.'

'Ah, but I didn't have coffee. . .' The big car swung off the road, into the drive of the Grange. 'Well, here we are at last! Let me give you a hand to get the dogs indoors and fed, will you?'

Kate, climbing down and already feeling the stiffness associated with using new muscles, shook her head.

'No, I can manage. You go and start soaking in a hot bath, then perhaps you'll be able to tackle your list tomorrow, after all.'

He laughed, but followed her into the kitchen.

'Come on, we shared the fun, now let me share the work. I'll open the tins whilst——'

'Hello, so you're back at last!'

Nell stood in the doorway, blinking owlishly at them, a glass in her hand. 'Sam and I were just having a sherry—want to join us?'

'No, thanks, I'm just helping Kate with the dogs,' Charles said before Kate could speak. 'And you'll have a full day tomorrow, Kate, so you'd best have an early night, too.'

Kate, judiciously measuring biscuits into the two earthenware dog dishes, smiled but shook her head at Nell.

'Sorry, Nell, no sherries for us. Who's Sam?'

'Oh, a guy I know,' Nell said vaguely. 'See you!'

She disappeared, and Kate and Charles continued to make the dogs' meals.

'I'm off now,' Charles said when the dishes were on the floor and the dogs oblivious of everything but eating. 'Thanks for a wonderful day, Kate.'

'I enjoyed every minute of it,' Kate said, moving over to the back door and holding it open for him. 'Goodnight, Charles.'

The surgeon moved towards the doorway, then turned to face her, putting his hands on her shoulders.

'Goodnight seems a bit remote. . .you sure you don't want to shake hands? Or something?'

Kate laughed.

'It depends what the "or something" is. . .'
she began, when Charles Patrick showed her.
Firmly he took her in his arms, and his mouth
moved in a series of small kisses across her
cheek, nose and chin, his lips finally fastening
on to hers.

Kate was first to pull back. Her senses swimming, her whole body announcing that it was
keen to continue, she still pulled away, hot,
excited. . .embarrassed. Good heavens, if Nell
should come back into the room whatever
would she think?

She voiced the thought, and Charles laughed
down on her, his arms still locked about her
slim body.

'What does it matter what anyone thinks, so
long as you and I enjoy it?' he said lazily. 'Oh,
Katie, Katie!'

He put his lips against her neck, moving it in
little kisses until his mouth found the V of her
shirt. Kate, trembling, knew what would come
next. . .already hands were pushing with impu-
dent confidence beneath the shirt, travelling
across her bare skin. . .

'*Goodnight*, Charles!' She tried to sound light-
hearted yet firm, but her voice wobbled. 'This is
not the place. . .'

He stepped back; she was still in his arms, but
now he was looking down at her, his eyes
sleepy, seductive.

'Confound it, nor the time. Goodnight, pretty

Kate; we shall continue this delightful interlude just as soon as I can arrange it!'

'It's all change today, then,' Kate remarked briskly as she and Sandra swished curtains back, turned mattresses, changed sheets and said goodbye to some of their small patients. 'I wonder who'll be driving us mad by teatime, Sandy?'

'They'll be Mr Patrick's operating list for Wednesday,' Sandra said prosaically. 'One of them's a gem, though—baby Trotter. She's got a hiatus hernia, poor mite; she was in once before, but it isn't getting better, so Mr Patrick's going to operate.'

'She'll be in a cubicle, of course,' Kate said thoughtfully. 'Hiatus hernias have to be nursed upright, otherwise you aggravate the condition, and that needs a cubicle, really.' She glanced up the ward. 'Who've we got left? Poor Suzy, of course, and little Alison, and Angela's still in her cubicle, and most of the others will be leaving either today or in the next few days.'

'So we'd better get a move on,' Sandra said. 'Otherwise the ward-round will come and we won't have the kids in their beds. Someone's done all the admissions, I suppose?'

'Sure to have,' Kate agreed. 'The new patients are in the playroom, getting to know one another. Can you finish off here, Sandra, while I check on the cubicles?'

'Sure, won't take me a moment,' Sandra said. 'Has baby Trotter arrived yet?'

'I think they're all here. I'd like a word with Angela's mother, though, before she goes off shopping.'

Accordingly she made her way up the ward and out of the doors at the end, turning into the short corridor lined with cubicles. Two student nurses and two pupil nurses were before her, changing babies, settling small patients and preparing the empty cots for their new occupants.

In Angela's cubicle a figure was bent over the bed, and Kate was about to walk past when a muffled shriek came from the room. Frowning, Kate opened the door.

'What's the matter? What's. . .? Dr Carruthers, what *are* you doing?'

Dr Carruthers straightened. The bedclothes were turned back and the cradle had been removed, and it appeared that the houseman had been examining Angela's small legs with their pitifully distended joints.

'I'm trying to test the mobility of the knee and ankle joints,' Dr Carruthers said. She turned a flushed face towards Kate, the eyes narrowed from annoyance. 'Though what business it is of yours, Nurse. . .'

'It's my business to nurse the patient and to care for her comfort,' Kate said quietly. 'Angela's limbs are acutely painful and should certainly not be subjected to mobility testing, as you call it. In fact the main aim of our nursing is to immobilise the joints at this stage, and make sure that the child suffers as little pain as possible.'

'In the interests of science—I'm writing a thesis on Still's disease—it's necessary for me to measure the amount of mobility left in the joints at this stage of the disease——' Dr Carruthers began, to be interrupted hotly by Kate.

'Would you please stand aside, Dr Carruthers? I have to replace the cradle and the covers. A draught can be dangerous in Angela's condition.'

'And suppose I refuse?'

'I'll fetch Sister, and she can ring Mr Patrick,' Kate said icily. 'It's up to you.'

The two young women stared at each other for a silent, tension-crackling moment, but Dr Carruthers's eyes were the first to fall. She moved back ungraciously, and Kate swept forward, picked up the cradle and placed it with infinite care over the child's legs. Then she drew the covers up, talking soothingly to Angela all the while.

When she turned away from the bed, her task completed, Dr Carruthers had vanished.

For the rest of the day Kate worked happily enough, but she could not help wondering what form Dr Carruthers's revenge would take, for it had speedily become plain that the young houseman was not one to take any sort of reprimand lying down. Kate had been getting on so well with Charles Patrick, though, that she could not think he would believe she had done wrong, so was not particularly perturbed when ward-round time approached. And, indeed, it seemed as though she was right, for the round went swimmingly, with Mr Patrick being friendly and sensible with the children and Dr Carruthers tagging along with the team, occasionally casting darkling glances at Kate.

But then they reached Angela's cubicle.

'Well, and how's the little one?' Mr Patrick asked Mrs Evans. Angela was awake and restless, bright spots of colour in her cheeks, and Mrs Evans was sitting well clear of the bed, holding her little girl's hand and reading to her from a book of fairy-stories.

'It's still really only affecting her knees, with her ankles tender, but by no means as bad as the knees,' Mrs Evans said timidly. 'She's being ever so good, Mr Patrick; such a good girl, aren't you, Angie?'

Angela tugged her mother's hand, and Mrs Evans turned obediently back to the book. 'And then the third little pig met a man carrying a load of bricks. . .'

Mr Patrick turned to Kate.

'How's the physio going, Staff?'

'Pretty well. The physiotherapist, Sally Dickinson, uses heat quite a lot, and wax baths, but Angela still cries, poor mite, because, of course, it's a very painful condition.'

Mr Patrick nodded, and would have passed on to the next cubicle but Dr Carruthers stopped him between the two.

'Oh, by the way, Charles, I tried to check the mobility of the child's joints this morning, for my thesis, but Nurse Reagan seemed to think I was acting out of turn. The child cried, of course. . .'

Mr Patrick turned and looked rather coolly at Kate. His brows rose.

'Well?'

'I assumed that Dr Carruthers didn't know, Mr Patrick, that's it's very important not to move or jostle a patient with Still's disease, far less to start trying to make the patient use the joints without first giving heat treatment of some description.'

'Very admirable, Nurse. But Dr Carruthers is writing her thesis on this disease and needs to make certain observations. She can scarcely wait for physiotherapy to start before she writes a word.'

'She could speak to Sally Dickinson. Sally uses measurements all the time to see how children are progressing,' Kate pointed out defensively.

All might have been well at that point. Mr Patrick was turning to go to the next cubicle, beginning to agree that this was a possible alternative, when Dr Carruthers murmured

something in his ear. Mr Patrick stopped in his
tracks as if he had been shot.

'Staff, am I to understand that you. . .? I'll see
you in Sister's office when the round is over.'

Agreeing, with a wooden countenance, to
meet him in Sister's office, Kate could have
screamed. That wretched Estelle Carruthers,
always making trouble! If only Charles had had
enough sense to see past her pretty face into the
devious mind behind it, but then he was a mere
man, and men were always swayed by feminine
beauty.

With this thought to comfort her Kate presently made her way to Sister's office, to find
Charles Patrick seated behind the desk, looking
grim.

'Staff, I've just been told that you more or less
threatened Dr Carruthers when you found her
trying to gauge the mobility in that child's
arthritic joints. What right do you think you
have to prevent a doctor from doing her job?'

'You aren't supposed to give a patient pain
without good reason, especially a small child,'
Kate said defensively. 'Angela's only five, and
Dr Carruthers waited until her mother had gone
down to the canteen for her lunch because she
knew very well that Mrs Evans wouldn't have
stood by and let her manipulate the child's legs
just for her wretched thesis!'

'Mrs Evans would probably have agreed,
knowing that a doctor was doing it for the

patient's good——' Mr Patrick was beginning, when Kate, flushed but determined, interrupted him.

'No, Mr Patrick, you're quite wrong. Mrs Evans is very shy but she's an intelligent woman; she's taken a keen interest in her daughter's treatment and she knows very well that only a physiotherapist should manipulate joints which are as swollen and painful as little Angela's knees. She would have stopped Dr Carruthers before she'd reduced the child to screams of pain.'

'Well, it's always dreadful to cause pain, but if Dr Carruthers's thesis helps to find a cure for Still's disease. . .'

Kate, regrettably, gave a snort.

'A cure? Dr Carruthers? Even if that were possible, though, I doubt that any caring parent would agree to their child's being experimented on in that way. So far as I'm concerned, sir, the end, in medicine, *never* justifies the means.'

'Hear, hear,' a voice from behind Kate's head commented. 'If I'd walked into that cubicle, Mr Patrick, your houseman would have been nursing more than hurt pride!'

Oh, bless you, Adèle, Kate thought gratefully; trust Sister to fly to your defence if she thinks you're in the right. Sister put a hand on her shoulder, her fingers gently reassuring.

'Ah, Sister! But did someone explain that Dr

Carruthers is writing a thesis on Still's disease for her——?'

'Mr Patrick, would *you* have tried to bend that child's knees when you were a houseman?'

There was a long and thoughtful pause before Charles Patrick spoke.

'No, Sister, I would not. I think we'll agree that, in this case, Dr Carruthers went a little too far. But she is a doctor, and Staff here——'

'Staff Nurse Reagan is an experienced and dedicated paediatric nurse,' Sister said gently. 'Dr Carruthers is merely serving a term with us. And I did tell you once, Mr Patrick, that she's already made mistakes in the past which could have been dangerous, even fatal. I don't want to have to ask for her to be transferred, but——'

'Look, part of it was my fault for not being more tactful,' Kate interrupted. 'If I was to apologise. . .'

'That would solve the problem,' Charles Patrick said, looking relieved. 'I gather it was your tone, Staff, which particularly upset Estelle, as well as the fact that you more or less ordered her to back off.'

'Then I'll tell her I'm sorry,' Kate said.

'Good. Well done. And in future, Staff, try not to throw your weight about quite so much. Everyone's life will be easier as a result.'

On the words Mr Patrick stood up. Kate, momentarily bereft of speech by the unfairness of the remark, was still trying to assemble a sentence to tell him what she thought without severing their relationship forever when he left the room, shutting the door far too firmly behind him. She and Adèle looked at one another.

'Well!' Kate said at last. 'Oh, Sister, how I would like to see Estelle Carruthers get her come-uppance!'

Sister smiled.

'She's riding for a fall,' she said. 'Let's hope she reaches it before I leave at the end of the month!'

'So, you see, I'm going to keep out of Charles Patrick's way for bit,' Kate concluded that evening as she and Nell prepared their evening meal. 'It's a real shame because we had a wonderful time last Thursday, but if he really thinks I should allow Estelle Carruthers to treat one of my patients like a *guinea-pig* then he can think again. No one should cause a child unnecessary pain, Nell, particularly a child suffering from a most painful and debilitating disease.'

'I agree,' Nell said, slicing cucumber. 'What exactly is Still's disease likely to do to the kid, though? I mean, will her little knees be deformed for life, or does she stand a chance of a complete recovery?'

'There's a good chance that Angela will make a complete recovery, because, although the illness is severe and came on suddenly, she's the right age to tackle it. They say the younger the patient the worse the prognosis. Oh, they rarely die of it, happily, but they can suffer from permanently deformed joints. But Angela's play-leader saw she was ill and got her into hospital at once—no messing about trying to cure her at home or hoping the fever would pass—and she was diagnosed here quickly, too.'

'Thanks to you,' Nell pointed out. 'Have you finished grating the cheese? Good, then I'll pop the garlic bread in the oven.'

'This was supposed to be a diet meal,' Kate grumbled, 'and you go putting hot garlic bread before me! Oh, how I long for will-power—and a twenty-two-inch waist, of course!'

'Have hot garlic bread instead. Shall we carry our plates through to the living-room or shall we eat here?'

'In view of the way Bonnie and Clyde dribble when they watch us eat, why don't we take it on to the terrace? It's a lovely warm evening.'

'Great,' Nell agreed at once. 'Except that, should the arch-enemy look out of his window and see us dining alfresco, there's nothing to stop him strolling down to join us.'

'Oh, damn, you're right. Shall we. . .? No! We'll sit on the terrace. After all, it's our ter-race—Maria never uses that part of the garden—and if Charles wants to come down he will have to be politely frozen off.'

So the two girls sat on the terrace with their salads and garlic bread, then with their strawberries dusted lightly with artificial sugar, and finally with their coffee. They talked about work, their wards, their patients and their own feelings and, though Kate tried very hard not to, they glanced, from time to time, up at the surgeon's flat.

But he did not come down, though once Kate could have sworn she saw his face at the window. And presently, the meal finished, they went indoors to wash up.

'I'll walk the dogs round the block for a quick twenty minutes,' Kate said when the meal had been cleared away. 'You lay the table for breakfast tomorrow, since we're both off. I shan't be long.'

'It's getting awfully dark; hadn't I better come with you?' Nell said dubiously, but Kate shook her head.

'What, with two great dogs to take care of me? I'll manage fine, really I will.'

'All right, if you're sure. I'll make us a hot drink to take to bed, though. Oh, by the way, Maria was in earlier, asking for you.'

Kate, shrugging herself into a light jacket, raised her brows.

'Really? What did she want?'

'I don't know. It couldn't have been much; she said she'd see you some other time. Don't be too long or your cocoa will get cold.'

'I won't. Come on Bonnie, Clyde. Walkies!'

It was a mild night, the stars above brilliant in the dark sky. Kate strode out, the two dogs pacing now beside her, now ranging ahead, for it was not necessary to keep them on the lead all the time, and once they reached a quiet side-road Kate usually released them for a run.

She was halfway along the side-road, which was tree-lined and unfrequented by much traffic, when she turned to see why Bonnie was lagging and saw a dark figure behind her. Frowning, she called the dog and then walked on. Someone else, like herself, exercising a dog? But although she could still see the figure now and then she could see no accompanying animal. Still, other people did take a walk last thing at night; doubtless the man—for it was certainly a man—was just taking a stroll before bed.

But when she reached the end of the road and went to turn back Kate found that her heart was thumping rather hard at the thought of the stranger, for this road was sparsely lit, with long distances between lamp standards, and what was more she could no longer see him. He might have turned back himself, but. . .well, suppose he was hiding behind one of the trees, or even in the shelter of the thick hedge?

Better safe than sorry, Kate concluded, fastening Bonnie's lead on. She would let Clyde continue to roam ahead but she would keep the gentler dog near her. No one, she was sure, would attack a woman with a large red setter on a lead!

Nevertheless, as she drew near to where a darker patch of shadow seemed to lurk she was conscious of a drying mouth. But she marched past, keeping her eyes to the front, and was relieved when Bonnie stared hard at the shadows but did not attempt to bark or to indicate in any way that danger threatened.

The experience, however, decided her to stick to the better-lit streets, so she walked the rest of the way on the main road, then turned and retraced her steps, to go back up the drive of the Grange once more.

The tall man had followed her, she realised as soon as she turned into her drive, for he was now no more than ten feet behind her. She walked up her drive and round the side, but she was so conscious, now, of pursuit that she dodged into the bushes, pulling both dogs in with her. How dared anyone follow her. . .? And he had; he was on the drive, actually trespassing!

He came past the bushes, moving quietly, just a tall, dark shape with the white blur of his face above a dark mac or coat of some description. Bonnie was on the lead still, but Kate had hold of Clyde's collar, and somehow, before she knew quite what was happening, the big dog had pulled free and was racing after the intruder.

Her cover broken, Kate followed, determined to order the man off her property. She raced round the corner, sure that the intruder would either flee or attempt to hide. . .and ran right into his arms!

'Clyde. . .here!' Kate shouted, trying to struggle free of the intruder's grip. But the man put her back from him, a hand on either shoulder.

'What's all this about? Kate?'

'Oh, Charles!' Kate said, too relieved that she was not about to be mugged or raped to remember their disagreement. 'Whatever were you doing, following me?'

'Following you? I wasn't. In fact, I was ahead of you, wasn't I? I came round the corner and Clyde chased after me, so I stopped, thinking he was on the loose, and the next thing I knew you'd flung yourself into my arms. . .very pleasant, if somewhat unexpected.'

'Oh!' Kate said, stepping back. Charles followed her, hands still warm round her shoulders. 'But you *did* follow me, Mr Patrick. . . I saw you as. . .as I turned into the drive, and earlier, too.'

'No, Miss Reagan, I didn't follow you, though I may well have come along the road after you. . .come to think of it, I did see someone with a dog ahead of me, but I was thinking hard and didn't look too closely. And, if I had been following you, how come I reached the yard first?'

'Because someone was following me throughout my walk,' Kate said obstinately. 'So when he. . .you. . .turned into the drive as well I hid in the bushes. I was going to confront you. . .him. . .and ask just what you thought you were doing.'

'I see, or I think I do. But I've just spent an evening at the theatre; I went straight to the show after I left the hospital and walked home because it's such a fine night and I've not had much exercise this week.'

'Really? Well, if it wasn't you, who was it? Because someone followed me all round, really they did.'

Charles shrugged.

'No idea. When you're with the dogs you should be safe enough.' He patted her shoulder and released her. 'But don't go out at nights without the dogs, unless you take someone with you. It just isn't safe, not even in Colney Bay.'

'He didn't believe me; he thought I was imagining it,' Kate said crossly to Nell later as the two of them sat and drank cocoa and ate shortbread biscuits. 'He was quite nice and polite about it, but I'm sure he thought I was making it up. Just as an excuse to dive into his arms, presumably,' she added bitterly.

'I don't see why; men do follow girls,' Nell

pointed out, crunching. 'Anyway, you've only his word for it that it wasn't him following you.'

'No, it's more than that. As we were walking across the terrace I asked him what he'd seen at the theatre, and he obviously thought I didn't believe him and was checking up. Because he told me the name of some play and added that if I still doubted his word I could check up with Estelle Carruthers, who was with him at the time!'

'And you didn't scratch his eyes out, or kick him in the essentials? What *savoir-faire*! What class!'

'I don't care whom he takes out,' Kate said untruthfully. 'He can take out the entire hospital staff if he likes—I'm better off without a man who's obviously crazy about someone else. I mean, he must be crazy about dear Estelle to defend her indefensible behaviour—and to dare to tell me that I'm throwing my weight about when all I'm doing is protecting a patient from that. . .that *creature*. . .is the end of our friendship so far as I'm concerned. Charles Patrick has cooked his goose.'

'And now he can eat it,' Nell added with a cackle. 'So you've taken your last hill-walking trip, have you?'

'With him I have! Did I tell you Bob Nettall asked me to go to the mountain zoo with him? I said I'd think about it and I jolly well have. I shall go, of course.'

'Of course,' Nell echoed. 'It doesn't matter to you if you never see Charles again, I dare say?'

'I wish I needed never see him again,' Kate said crossly. 'But unfortunately, since I've no intention of leaving Pantomine Ward, meetings are unavoidable. But I said right from the start that meeting socially was a mistake, and haven't I been proved right?'

'Absolutely,' Nell said soothingly. 'And now can we go to bed? There's another long day ahead of us tomorrow.'

'I'm too cross to sleep,' Kate said. 'What a disastrous evening! If *only* I hadn't accused him of following me! If only I'd not hidden in those bushes!'

'I wonder who was following you, though,' Nell said thoughtfully. 'You said the dogs didn't make a fuss, so it must have been someone they know—Clyde's all right, but Bonnie's very nervy at night, isn't she?'

'Yes, she is,' Kate said, frowning thoughtfully. 'Well, it wasn't Maria. . .Oh, I was so *sure* it was Charles!'

'Wishful thinking,' Nell said, laughing at her friend's scowl. 'Come on, Kate, be honest—you really do like the guy!'

'Yes, sometimes. But I like to like the people I like all the time. . .Gosh, what a sentence!'

'It's the sort of sentence that only gets said when you're fagged to death,' Nell said soothingly. 'Come on, bed! I bet you'll sleep like a log tonight!'

Kate complied and the two girls went up to bed. But, in Kate's case at least, not to sleep. She lay awake for a long time, not only annoyed with Charles, who had so little discernment that he could not only defend Estelle Carruthers but could also take her to the theatre, but annoyed with herself, too. Why had she not put Clyde on the lead and faced the man, in the light of the street-lamps? Now the fact that she had been followed would prey on her mind, when in reality it was probably just a neighbour out for a stroll, with no interest in her whatsoever. Someone who knew the dogs well, but had not yet had much opportunity to get to know Kate and Nell.

And as for Charles Patrick—let him take horrible Estelle to the theatre; he would soon realise that Kate had better things to do with her time than pine for him!

CHAPTER SIX

'My last week!' Adèle put a hand in the small of her back and got up off her chair. 'I shan't be sorry, either. I'm getting slow and I tire rather easily but, thanks to the way you've learned the job, I'll be leaving here knowing you fit in and can handle the people as well as the work.'

The two women were in Sister's office, Adèle watching while Kate did some paperwork, but now Kate put down her pen and yawned.

'Don't think I'm bored, I'm just not used to *quite* so much administrative work, so I get fidgety quickly,' she said. 'As for fitting in, Adèle, that's been as much the staff as me. They're all so friendly and co-operative—with one notable exception.'

'Dr Carruthers,' Sister nodded. 'But she doesn't like anyone who gets attention away from her, and because you're a newcomer, and young to be Sister of a big ward like this, she's jealous. However, she'll move on and with a bit of luck the next houseman assigned to Pantomine will be a little nicer and a lot more efficient.'

'But Charles Patrick won't be moving on,' Kate said gloomily. 'He doesn't approve of me either.'

'Charles? Nonsense, of course he does! But he's used to women adoring him and agreeing with him and, in some cases, practically falling at his feet—he's spoilt, in other words. He was wrong to criticise your work and to expect you to simply accept all his strictures without arguing, but when you're sister you'll find him a lot more reasonable. He's certainly never disagreed with me over how my babies should be treated.'

'I hope you're right,' Kate said doubtfully. 'But I'm always the soul of politeness towards him on the ward.'

'And off it?'

Kate grinned. 'That's a different story. Have you heard about the dahlia bed?'

Sister laughed. 'Just rumours. Come into the kitchen and we'll make coffee and you can tell me the truth.'

'There isn't all that much to tell,' Kate admitted. 'Except that Mr Patrick. . .only he's Charles, out of work. . .said he'd like to help in the garden, so he took over one of the big beds, said he would soon have it planted up with dahlias and by autumn it would be a picture.'

'And what happened?'

'Clyde happened. Poor fellow, he saw Charles digging and weeding and having a wonderful time and decided he ought to do his bit. So, when Charles had finished and gone indoors to scrub up, Clyde put in some serious work and dug out all the tubers which Charles had so lovingly buried.'

'That's enough to annoy a saint,' Adèle pointed out. 'What happened, though? Couldn't you have replaced them, and Charles none the wiser? For the sake of peace, mainly,' she added.

'I would have, except that Charles found out first, while I was cooking supper, and Clyde seems to have rather strange tastes. Unless there's some doggy edict which says what you dig up you must devour.'

'He didn't! You mean he ate the dahlia tubers?'

Kate nodded vigorously as the two of them entered the kitchen.

'I fear so. I hope they gave him tummy ache, because Charles gave me a most awful telling-off, and I told him I didn't own the dogs, and he said I did now, and harsh words were exchanged, with poor Nell standing by trying to pour oil on troubled waters whenever there was a gap in the acrimonious conversation. . .at one stage our beloved boss actually turned to her and told her to pipe down! Poor Nell nearly hit him!'

'Gracious,' Adèle said mildly. 'It's not a bit like Charles, you know. He's very suave and good-tempered as a rule.'

'Only because, as a rule, no one ever crosses him,' Kate pointed out. 'I decided a while back to treat him as though he were just another tenant while we're at the Grange, and he doesn't like it one bit. But it's doing him good, you know. He complained about our music centre the other evening, said he couldn't hear his own stuff for the din we were making, and I was *most* obliging, and turned it down at once. And when I offered him a coffee and a slice of chocolate gâteau he accepted and came and perched on the kitchen table and chatted for a good half-hour.'

'And you try to say he doesn't approve of you,' Adèle said, rummaging in the biscuit tin. 'I never said he was an easy man, Kate, but it seems to me he's easier with you than anyone else. I can't see him sitting on my kitchen table eating cake and chatting.'

'He isn't a tenant in your house, though; he'd be a guest,' Kate said. 'Are you still refusing sugar in coffee, or will you have just a half-spoonful?'

'No, none, thanks,' Adele said firmly. 'We'll take these back to the office and then you can go on the ward. I know you're longing to do so.'

'I enjoy nursing more than admin,' Kate agreed. 'Have you seen baby Potter this morning? She's a darling, isn't she? And she responded marvellously to surgery.'

'It's a tricky operation,' Sister said. 'But, if anyone can get it right first go, Charles can.'

'True. I spoke to Sister Mainwaring, from

Theatre, and she said he went in through the abdomen, replaced the stomach in the abdominal cavity, repaired the defect in the diaphragm muscles, and baby Potter was on her way to Recovery in not much more than an hour.'

'Yes, he's a first-rate surgeon,' Sister agreed. 'I often wish he had a family of his own, though. It would make his approach to the little ones a good deal gentler and more understanding, I'm sure.'

Kate, carrying the tray, pushed the door of the office ajar and put her burden down on the desk, then helped herself to a cup of coffee and two biscuits and sat down in the chair she had previously occupied. Adèle, with a sigh, sat down beside her.

'Gentler and more understanding, Adèle? But I thought Charles was a prince compared to his predecessor!'

'He is. But that doesn't mean he couldn't be even better. He believes that if pain is necessary to cure a child then pain should be administered. He doesn't look round to see how that pain could be avoided and the child cured just the same.'

'The end justifying the means,' Kate nodded. 'But he's coming round, Adèle. He wanted a skin sample from little Roddy Transom to see just why he had that horrific eczema, and he was just going to take it, as though Roddy were immune from pain because he's only nine months. But Mrs Transom and I persuaded him that Roddy would benefit from an anaesthetic, and he agreed, albeit reluctantly.'

'Men don't have our imaginations,' Adèle said sagely. 'Just you let someone try to take a skin sample from this little one. . .' she patted her stomach '. . .without an anaesthetic and see what happens!'

Kate finished her coffee and replaced the cup on the saucer, then stood up.

'I think that's how all the mothers feel,' she observed. She checked her uniform with the swift downward glance which so many nurses had brought to perfection, and set off for the door, saying over her shoulder, 'It's time baby Potter was fed and changed, and that is a job I like to supervise.'

Baby Potter was in a cubicle with Nurse Sarah Fields. Sarah was wandering round with the feed, clean disposable nappies and clothing all laid out and ready, while baby Potter was just waking from slumber and looking about her, the smile which had so endeared her to the nurses already in evidence.

'Everything all right. Sarah?' Kate asked, closing the cubicle door behind her. 'Are you hungry, then, Dolly?'

Baby Potter, hearing herself addressed, gurgled adorably, and Kate took her carefully from her bed and propped the child in a sitting position in her arm, then reached for the feed.

'Are you watching, Sarah? Never forget it's very important to let a child with any sort of oesophagus trouble take a feed very slowly, because that's the best way to keep the nourishment in its stomach. Also, of course, since the feed has been thickened it will take the baby longer to drink.'

'Yes, Kate, I'll remember. And she has to be burped very gently, and not over the shoulder.'

'Good. In a moment I'll hold Dolly upright against me, and I'll very gently rub her back and hope that wind will come up and no feed.'

'Though most babies sick a bit of milk back,' Sarah observed, watching baby Potter's single-minded sucking. 'My cousin's got a baby the same age as this one and he sicks up when he brings up wind.'

'True. But we don't want any sort of vomiting from baby Potter, with a hernia repair only a couple of days old. And when she's taken her feed and brought up any wind then we'll change her, still in a sitting position.'

Kate looked down at the small, absorbed face in the crook of her arm. This little mite would never look back, now that her hernia had been expertly mended. But what of the others? Poor little Angela with her painful joints, and Suzy, who had been bored for most of her enforced stay on the ward. Their memories of hospital could not be pleasant ones. All you could do, really, was try to minimise the fear and the pain, and use every endeavour to see that the children in your charge were happy.

Paediatric nurses are awfully lucky, Kate thought. How many oher jobs give girls a chance to work with children who need them and are ready to love them? When things go well we see a healthy child take up his or her life again, and when things go badly at least we make our small patients as comfortable and as happy as we possibly can. She looked down at baby Potter's face, the expression on it one of total satisfaction. What other job let you cuddle and love a tiny baby, gave you the expertise to help that baby and see it grow strong again? It really *is* a wonderful job, Kate told herself. I wouldn't swap with anyone else in the world right now!

It had been a hot summer, and when Kate finished work that night she considered whether to abandon all her plans and go down to the beach first for a swim. But conscience won. She had planned to go home, get soup and salad, do a bit of gardening and then take the dogs out and, since Nell was going to a party with Richard, she really should do as she had intended.

But she missed the bus, of course. Deciding it was too hot to even consider walking, she mooched around near the bus-stop and was looking wistfully into a shop window displaying various icecream-making machines when she heard her name called.

'Kate! Hey Katie!'

Turning, she saw Bob Nettall waving to her from his MG Midget. It had the hood down and looked racy and exciting, though Kate knew very well that it was a dozen years old and should, according to its owner, have been pensioned off years before.

'Oh, hello, Bob,' Kate said, walking over to him. 'Where are you off to?'

'Anywhere. Want a lift? It's such a lovely evening that I thought I'd go for a spin, and then I saw you, and. . .well, are you doing anything this evening?'

Bob and Kate had been out twice, and Kate had to admit that she had thoroughly enjoyed Bob's company, though only as a friend. Sex appeal, she thought ruefully, only seems to work for me when it's attached to bad-tempered paediatricians who fancy beautiful but nasty housemen! Or perhaps I should say housewomen, she thought, with an inward giggle.

'This evening?' Kate pretended to consider. 'Having a salad and then doing some gardening before I take the dogs out.'

'Oh, be a sport and come out with me instead,' Bob coaxed. 'Registrars lead such dull lives! Look, tell you what, I'll take you out to Stanley's for a slap-up dinner, and then I'll do some gardening with you. Isn't that a generous offer?'

'Sounds good,' Kate admitted. 'Where is Stanley's?'

Bob grinned guiltily.

'I was hoping you'd never ask! It isn't the most exclusive night-spot, nor perhaps the most expensive, but the food's good and——

'It's that big fish and chip café down by the pleasure beach,' Kate interrupted. 'I thought it was just take-away.'

'They do have a couple of tables,' Bob protested. He got out and helped Kate into the passenger-seat. 'Anyway, fish and chips is a slap-up meal when you're as poor as I am! Going to be a good sport?'

'I suppose so,' Kate said, settling back in her seat. 'For a lift home I'm quite willing to eat fish and chips, actually. And why is the dangerously attractive young paediatric registrar at a loose end, may I ask?'

Bob put the car into gear and they drew away from the kerb.

'It's a beautiful evening and I'm sick of studying,' he said. 'Besides, my landlady does the worst meal of the week on a Tuesday, and that means not just nasty but inedible. Slimy cabbage, bones boiled in salted water with a few bits of carrot and onion floating in it, and a thing she calls *crème* surprise, which means a beastly watery pink blancmange.'

'It's your own fault for going into lodgings instead of having a place of your own,' Kate pointed out righteously. 'What you need is somewhere with a little kitchen so you can——'

'Warm up fish and chips in my own little oven,' Bob finished for her, grinning. 'I'm no cook. No, what I really need is a pretty, efficient nurse to come and live with me, darn my socks, cook my meals and see to my creature comforts. Any offers?'

'I don't mind warming up the fish and chips and making a baked Alaska for pudding,' Kate said, 'but I draw the line at your socks.'

'What about creature comforts?'

'If I knew what they were I'd draw the line at them, too,' Kate said positively. 'Ah, here's Stanley's—can I have a huge piece of haddock and just a few chips, please?'

'Why not make a pig of yourself and have curry sauce and mushy peas as well?' Bob said persuasively. 'I shall—I'm starving hungry. We rich young registrars like to throw our money about when we treat a girl!'

'A girl? A sister. . .well, I'll be a sister next Monday,' Kate reminded him. 'Not that we rich young sisters have much money to throw about, come to think.'

'I shall always think of you as a sister,' Bob said, grinning as he got out of the car. 'Want to come in and choose?'

Presently, armed with their newspaper parcels, they got back in the car and very soon were turning into the driveway of the Grange. Bob, who had dropped Kate off once or twice but had never been inside the house, followed her across the yard, heavily laden, expressing a good deal of interest in the flat.

'And I've never met the dogs, either,' he observed as Kate unlocked. 'Wonder what they'll think of me?'

Kate smiled. The dogs' ecstatic welcome was something which had to be endured rather than enjoyed and she was quite looking forward to seeing how Bob took it! But to her suprise no dogs bounded out as she threw open the door, and there was no sound of scratching or whimpering from behind the door leading into the rest of the flat, either.

'They aren't here,' she announced, turning to Bob. He staggered past her and dumped the newspaper parcels on the kitchen table. 'Oh, perhaps they're still in the stables.'

But they were not. The stables were empty and, when Kate looked at the hook where their leads always hung, it was empty too.

'I suppose Nell came home first, after all, and decided to take the dogs out,' she said rather doubtfully. Nell did her share of the gardening and helped with the housework, but rarely exercised the dogs, claiming, with a certain amount of truth, that they seemed to like and obey Kate but had no time for herself.

'Or are they with Maria?' Bob—who had heard all about the set-up at the Grange—suggested. But Maria never took the dogs out, though Kate did pick up the telephone and ask her.

'No, Maria hasn't seen them, but she thinks possibly Mr Patrick came in and took them,' she said, going to the pantry for vinegar, tomato sauce and salt. 'Maria heard a masculine voice in here earlier. . .hey, that can't be right! Charles doesn't have a key for this place, though he could have taken them from the stable block.'

'Maria must have meant she heard a voice from the stables, then,' Bob said. He unwrapped the first parcel and helped himself to a succulent chip. 'Crumbs, these are piping hot—no need for oven-warming this evening!'

'Stop eating them before they're even set out on the plates,' Kate said severely. 'Goodness, I didn't realise how hungry I was until now! I've put the kettle on; do you want some bread and butter with them?'

'No need,' Bob said with a full mouth. 'What about that pudding you promised me?'

'I'll make pancakes instead,' Kate said soothingly. 'No time to create a baked Alaska now.'

The two of them ate their food, cleared away and then went companionably into the garden. The lawn wanted mowing and the edges needed a trim, to say nothing of the vegetable garden, a brain-child of Charles Patrick's, which had suddenly begun to flourish a fine crop of thistles. Bob got out the electric mower and began to steer it over the grass and Kate put on gardening gloves and tackled the thistles, and they talked whenever they were near enough—hospital gossip mostly, about their colleagues, their patients and mutual friends in the hospital system.

Kate was rather enjoying herself, when she saw Charles Patrick's car draw up outside the back door. She got to her feet, knowing she was flushed and rather dirty, but determined to ask him how he had managed to get the dogs out of her flat. If he had a key then, boss or no boss, he must give it up at once.

She approached the car, words already on her lips, but they died when she saw he was alone.

'Evening, Kate,' Charles said cheerfully. 'Who's that mowing the lawn? Richard?'

'Bob Nettall,' Kate said quickly. 'Charles, where are the dogs?'

'Bob?' The friendly smile was wiped off the surgeon's face as if by magic. 'What's *he* doing here?'

'Mowing the lawn. Charles, why did you take the dogs? I didn't know you could get into the garden flat.'

'Why is my registrar cutting the lawn? Damn it, Kate, that's my job!'

Kate blinked. Charles had certainly cut the lawn a couple of times, but she could not recall any great enthusiasm, nor that he had thrust her roughly from the lawn-mower when he had seen her toiling up and down the grass!

'Your job? Well, you can go and tell Dr Nettall to have a rest while you take over if you like, but I *still* want to know how you got Bonnie and Clyde out of my flat when the doors were all locked and the windows closed.'

For the first time she could see he was listening to her. He stared, a little frown appearing between his straight dark brows.

'The dogs? I haven't seen them. Aren't they indoors?'

'This is absurd,' Kate said helplessly. 'I can't believe that anyone would steal two very large, very hungry red setters! There has to be an explanation—I suppose Nell must have taken them.'

'But Nell never takes the dogs out,' Charles objected. 'Still, I suppose. . .'

A white van, approaching along the drive, put a stop to conjecture.

'Nell,' Kate called as soon as the van was within hailing distance, 'have you seen the dogs?'

'No. Why, have they got out? Well, they won't run far,' Nell said, jumping out of the van. 'I've asked Richard home for some tea. . .you've had yours, I suppose?'

'Yes. Nell, the dogs are missing; they must have been stolen! Their leads are gone, and yet the flat was locked up. . . I suppose I'd better ring the police.'

Bob finished the final strip of lawn and came over to them. A fine perspiration bedewed his brow.

'Evening, Charles,' he said cheerfully. 'Did you take the dogs for a walk?'

'No, I did not!' the surgeon shouted. 'What's going on? Why does everyone keep accusing *me* of taking the bloody animals?'

'Come into the kitchen and I'll put the kettle on and we'll explain everything,' Kate said soothingly. She turned to Nell. 'Do you and Richard want to come along as well, or are you yearning for privacy?'

Nell, resplendent in cream silk with a pattern of scarlet poppies, beckoned Richard out of the van.

'We were on our way to a party when we suddenly realised we hadn't eaten and didn't know whether the party included a buffet, so we nipped back here,' she explained. 'I must say, I'm intrigued by all this talk of theft. Or should I say dog-napping? What will we do if a letter arrives with Bonnie's dear ear attached?'

'It isn't funny,' Kate snapped, marching into the kitchen with the other four trailing behind, and filling the kettle with such vigour that the floor and her person were both liberally splashed. 'I'm telling you, someone got in here and stole the dogs.'

'But, my dear Kate, thieves don't steal *dogs*,' Charles said mildly. 'A television set or your jewels, yes. But I've never heard of a dog-theft.'

'Nor had I until now. But we don't have valuables, Nell and I, and the dogs are worth a bit—you said so yourself—so what other explanation can there be? The doors were locked, Maria confirmed that the dogs were shut indoors and not in the stables, the leads have gone. . .it must be theft!'

'Animal rights movement,' Bob suggested brightly. 'Thought you didn't treat Bonnie and Clyde properly so they took matters into their own hands.'

The kettle boiled and Kate made tea while Nell got out the fruit cake she had made the previous weekend.

'Do you know what I'm beginning to think?' Kate said, pouring tea into five mugs. 'I think the dogs have been reclaimed, not stolen. When I was followed the other night neither dog made a fuss. I bet it was Maria's tenants, planning to grab the dogs then! That was why they didn't bark or make a fuss today either, but just let the chap walk away with them. The people who had the flat before us did a moonlight flit, Maria said, which means they certainly didn't hand in their keys.'

There was a thoughtful silence while everyone digested this latest suggestion.

'I think you're right,' Charles said at last, taking the proffered mug of tea and perching on the kitchen table as he had done on his last visit. 'Very bright, Kate—so that's one problem solved. I suppose they couldn't just ask for the dogs back; they owed Maria money, after all. Well, at least in future a tuber planted will remain in the earth to flower.'

'Is that all you can think about?' Kate demanded. 'What worries me now is that someone's got a key to this flat, someone pretty damned unreliable, who might walk in just when they please and murder us in our beds.'

'You've got a point, Kate. Shall I change the lock for you?' Bob offered.

'It's all right, Nettall,' Charles said, rather coolly, Kate thought. 'I'm on the spot and I've got a spare lock and tools and so on in the flat upstairs; I'll fix it. I dare say you'll want to be getting home.'

Kate was about to protest that it was Bob's business when he left and nothing to do with Charles Patrick, when she saw that Bob was looking self-conscious, even slightly uncomfortable. There was no need for such feelings, of course, except that for reasons of his own Charles had decided to act like a dog with a bone. . .Kate being the bone. . .and was glaring jealously at the other dog who had dared to glance at his property. It's no business of Charles Patrick's whom I bring home for an impromptu supper or whom, for that matter, I spend the night with, Kate told herself. But Bob can clearly see the way to his boss's heart is *not* through flirting with me, and, since it's important to have a good atmosphere at work, then it behoves Bob to take himself quietly off. And, as Kate knew very well that, much though she liked Bob, she had no interest in him in a romantic sense, there was no point in her trying to delay the young registrar simply to prove a point.

Accordingly, she waved Bob off and then returned to the kitchen. Nell, now wearing a light coat over her party dress, was drinking the last of her tea and Richard was tapping his car keys impatiently on the jamb of the back door. Clearly the two of them were about to leave at last for their party.

'Kate, love, I'm awfully sorry but if you do manage to fix a new lock this evening, do you think you could leave a key out for me? We won't be much after midnight. Unless you want to wait up for me, of course.'

'It's all right, I won't lock you out,' Kate said rather wearily. It was already ten o'clock and the last thing she felt like doing was sitting around by herself for two hours. Charles, still perched on the kitchen table, swinging his legs and eating fruitcake and looking totally at home, told Nell to enjoy herself in an avuncular tone, waited until the van had purred away down the drive, and then dusted his hands together and slid off the table.

'Well now, I'll leave you for five minutes while I find the lock and some tools. You can put the kettle on again if you like.'

'It's very good of you,' Kate said with only moderate gratitude. She was beginning to wonder if she was making a fuss about nothing—if the dog owners had come back and taken their own dogs what was wrong with that? Sure, they owed Maria money, but that did not make them thieves who would break into the flat for any purpose other than to retrieve—ha-ha—their retrievers! When she thought about it it occurred to her that if they intended to steal they would have done so earlier, when they took the dogs. She and Nell had not been in the flat long enough to have many possessions but, although she went and looked in her bedroom while Charles returned to his flat for the necessary tools, it was easy to see that she had not been robbed in her absence.

When the kettle boiled a second time she made cocoa and got out the shortbread, and presently Charles came in, flushed and triumphant, and duly fixed a new lock to the back door and clicked the Yale down on the front one.

'You're safe as houses now,' he observed, sliding the catch back and forth a couple of times to see that it ran smoothly. 'But if you want me to stay. . .'

'No, thank you,' Kate said hastily, and saw that he was grinning at her with the wicked, charming expression which she had not seen much of lately. It was odd how very human he could be at home, and how positively inhuman he could be at work, always trying to put her in her place and take her down a peg or two.

'No? Quite sure? Very well, then, back to my lonely couch.' He stood up, towering over her. 'Sweet dreams, and call if you want me.'

Kate hurried to the back door to wave him off and walked right into his arms. He kissed her nicely, then with somewhat less niceness and a good deal more passion. He took advantage of the fact that Kate was suddenly feeling lonely and unsure of herself, gathering her into a warm embrace, letting his lips stray across her face in small, gentle kisses before homing in on her mouth and suddenly, hungrily, deepening the kiss, his hands demanding, his body hard against hers.

Kate could have wept. She wanted—how much she wanted—to let him love her, but it was sheer foolishness because tomorrow, at work, he would be as nasty as ever—nastier, probably, because he would begin to guess how she felt about him, realise that he did have the power to make or break.

'Goodnight, Charles,' she said dismissively as

soon as she was able to speak. 'And thanks very much for fixing the lock; I feel safer, now.'

Her boss sighed deeply, releasing her, looking down at her with a rueful grin.

'You've never been in more danger,' he remarked. 'Why don't we adjourn to your living-room couch for an exchange of mutual comfort?'

'Or you could invite me up to see your etchings,' Kate said pensively. 'It's bedtime, Charles, and I'm very tired.'

'I know it's bedtime, but I didn't like to suggest we adjourned to——'

'I should hope not,' Kate said severely, but with a thumping heart. He really must like her, to joke and fool around like this. . .but she still did not trust his feelings not to change over-night. 'You've got a list tomorrow, and I've got a full ward. Goodnight.'

'Oh, all right, I'll go. But I'll be back.' Unexpectedly he put out a hand, tilting her chin, his expression softening. 'Poor kid, you really *are* tired! Off you go, then.'

He looked at me as though he really cared, Kate thought wonderingly as she climbed into bed. I think he probably does care, only in not quite the way I'd like.

It was odd, but somehow her worries over who had taken the dogs and why seemed suddenly insignificant and she fell asleep quite quickly, scarcely waking when Nell came in and called out she was home.

CHAPTER SEVEN

NEXT morning, with Kate rushing to make some toast while Nell poured two cups of tea, the girls tried once more to make sense of the theft—if such it was—of the dogs.

'I just hope the thieves fed them both last night,' Kate said. 'Because I didn't. Oh, dear, I've grown awfully fond of those great dopey dogs, but I suppose they've gone for good.'

'Perhaps they'll run home, like the animals in that film. . .what was it called. . .oh, yes, *Incredible Journey*,' Nell suggested brightly. 'But, if they don't, at least you won't have to slog round the countryside with them all through the winter; you know you'd not been looking forward to that.'

'I'd got used to the idea,' Kate said truthfully. 'It's been awfully good for me, walking the dogs.'

'We could always buy a puppy, I suppose,' Nell suggested, buttering toast. 'We'd best get a move on, Katie, or we'll miss the bus.'

It seemed strange to eat breakfast and go, without first exercising the dogs for ten minutes, seeing that they had water down and dry dog-biscuits, and then waving goodbye to the two faces pressed close to the glass panes in the back door as they peered hopefully out after the two girls.

'Strange but pleasant,' Nell said when Kate voiced the thought. 'Oh, the dogs were all right, but they were a responsibility and one I could get along without.'

'I know what you mean,' Kate conceded. The bus arrived and they both jumped on board. 'But one day I'll have a dog of my own which no one will want to steal. . .only not while I'm working full-time. Perhaps when I get married. . .'

'I thought you were going to be a career nurse,' Nell teased as they pushed their way up the crowded bus. 'I thought a husband and a family were way down your list.'

'So did I,' Kate admitted. 'But people change, and it seems I have. Perhaps other people's babies aren't enough for me, after all.'

Nell turned to stare at her friend.

'Babies? You want babies? Heavens, girl, you must be in love!'

She laughed and Kate laughed too, though a trifle hollowly. Ever since the moment when Charles Patrick had held her in his arms and she had known how much she wanted his love-making to continue she had been fighting her own feelings, and until now she had believed she was winning. Away from work he was amusing company, a delightful companion, someone to whom she could talk freely, with whom she could feel totally at ease. At work he was a first-rate surgeon, someone whose sensitivity was growing as he became more aware of the needs of the little children in his care. But— and it was a big but—he had defended Estelle Carruthers's indefensible behaviour and he had taken the young doctor to the theatre, so it was pointless, and might prove painful, for Kate to let herself dream of a future in which she and Charles shared more than just a working relationship.

Nevertheless, she could not help her mind playing with a certain delightful picture of herself, smiling mistily down at the tiny baby in her arms while the father—tall, dark and handsome—looked down with pride and possessiveness at the pair of them. And the father had navy blue eyes and a wicked, charming smile!

Days on Pantomine Ward were often busy, but this one, Kate told herself as she and Sarah worked on a newly admitted patient, was going to be busier than usual. The child had complained of severe abdominal pains which the admitting doctor thought might be either acute appendicitis or even meningitis, since the symptoms were often similar. This would mean that they would need to be prepared for a neurological examination which would involve a lumbar puncture so that the cerebrospinal fluid might be examined, as well as throat swabs, blood samples and possibly even a chest X-ray.

The patient was a small boy of eight, who was being nursed in a cubicle with an anxious mother in attendance. Kate had done her best to be reassuring but there was no doubt that the little boy was very ill. When Dr Carruthers had tried to examine him earlier he had resisted, curling up into a tight little ball of agony and moaning that she hurt him, hurt him!

Bob Nettall˙ had had better luck, largely because he had talked soothingly to little Carl and had made sure his hands were warm before they touched the child's rigid abdomen. Estelle Carruthers had ignored Kate's bowl of hot water and had been sent out of the cubicle by the registrar when he arrived. Bob had pulled a face at her departing back and told Kate he thanked God that teacher's pet only had another three weeks on the ward.

'Just let's make sure she's kept clear of this little lad until he's better,' he said as he gave instructions for the various tests to be done. 'Supervise this lot yourself, Kate, won't you?'

Kate promised, and now she and Sarah were tackling the work. Various doctors and specialists came and went, and at ten o'clock promptly Charles Patrick arrived, still in his coat, with a freshness about him which told the harassed nurses that he had come straight up to the ward from the car park.

'Right, old chap, let's have a look at you,' he said cheerfully. 'Test results out yet, Kate?'

'Not yet. Sarah's slipped out to get some hot water for your hands, sir.'

'Oh, right. Now, Carl, you tell me about this pain of yours. When did it start?'

The day, which had begun with Carl's emergency admission, continued to be an unusually busy one. By lunchtime Kate was really looking forward to her break so was not best pleased to find herself hailed urgently by one of the student nurses.

'Oh, Kate, could you come? They've sent a child up from Cas, emergency admission. Dr Nettall's down in Theatre with Mr Patrick, but Dr Carruthers has been sent for and won't be long. Kate, the little boy's in an awful state; he's still in his swimsuit, but——'

'Where is he? What's the diagnosis?' Kate said crisply, following Jane who was all but tugging at her apron. 'Ah, the bed with curtains round. . .Here's Dr Carruthers.'

The three of them went into the curtained-off bed area together, to find the child, a little boy of about six, flat on his back, his head propped at an unnatural angle by the pillows and his skin cyanosed, the lips blue. A woman, clearly his mother, hung over him, wringing her hands and talking rapidly.

'It's all right, Stevie, you'll be fine presently;

someone will fetch a doctor and. . .' She broke off as the three women entered. 'There you are, you see? You'll be better in a brace of shakes.'

'If you'd wait outside while I conduct my examination. . .' Dr Carruthers began, but Kate, determined to be tactful, touched her arm.

'It's a bad asthma attack; he'll do better with his mother here to calm him,' she murmured. Dr Carruthers gave her a scornful look but bent over the bed.

'Now what brought this on?' she said. 'Have you been out in the fields, playing near hedge blossom, or farm animals?'

The child was too intent on the struggle for breath to answer her, and Kate went to the head of the bed and lifted the child bodily, sitting him up to ease his breathing. She reached behind him for the pillows and piled them up across the child's lap.

'Lean forward, love; it will help,' she said gently. And then, seeing that Dr Carruthers was about to start filling in admission forms, addressed Jane in an urgent under-voice. 'Bring oxygen and get intravenous infusion set up,' she said. 'Dr Carruthers will want them presently.'

Jane bustled off, and Dr Carruthers proceeded to try to sound the child's chest and began to ask him questions which he was in no state to answer. When the mother tried to answer for him, however, Dr Carruthers tutted at her, telling her in her sharp voice to let the boy answer for himself.

'He can't, doctor,' Kate said in a low voice, doing her best to conceal her impatience with the houseman. 'He's too ill. Ah, here's Jane with the oxygen; let's get that in place right away.'

'Not until I've completed the admission,' the doctor said as Jane came through the curtains with the equipment. 'Besides it will frighten him, the mask and so on, to say nothing of the infusion set. Children hate needles.'

'We'll set up the equipment while you complete the admission,' Kate said soothingly, though inside she was seething. Three more weeks of Dr Carruthers was three weeks too many so far as she was concerned. 'Bring the cylinder round this side, Jane.'

Working swiftly, the two nurses had Stevie on oxygen and the infusion ready before Dr Carruthers had completed the admission; Kate was, in fact, about to go in search of the registrar when she heard voices, and the curtains were parted so that Dr Nettall and Charles Patrick could enter the small enclosure.

Dr Carruthers looked up and smiled brightly at the paediatrician.

'Oh, Charles, I'm glad you've arrived. I was just about——'

'Who set up the oxygen?' Mr Patrick said briskly. 'And who put up the infusion set?'

Before Kate could plead guilty Estelle Carruthers, her eyes bright with spite, was in full voice.

'Well, Charles, it most certainly wasn't *me*—I know better than to start treating a patient before a doctor has done a proper diagnosis, but Nurse Reagan had to interfere, and——'

'Well done, Kate,' Mr Patrick said genially. 'You're worth your weight in gold! Off you go, Estelle, if you've finished the admission.'

'I was about to get oxygen ready on stand-by, and the infusion set up, when Nurse Reagan interfered,' Dr Carruthers said, her face turning an unbecoming beetroot shade. 'She piled pillows on the poor child's stomach, she——'

'Estelle, you're simply proving with every word you utter that experience in a children's ward is worth years of examinations,' Mr Patrick said, quite gently, Kate thought. 'Nurse Reagan acted properly and promptly, as, it seems to me, she always does.' He turned back to the patient. 'Now, my lad, I think we'll give you a quick injection which will make you feel very much better. . .Kate, I'll need. . .'

Kate nodded contentedly as her boss told her to fetch an anti-spasmodic drug for Stevie. Sister had always said Mr Patrick would see through Estelle one day; she was just glad that Estelle's dislike of herself had moved her to be so overtly spiteful. When she returned with the required drug she handed it over to the paediatrician, feeling that one enormous obstacle to her success as Sister on the ward had been overcome before her new status had actually taken effect. She would no longer have to fight the surgeon's belief in every word his houseman said, nor struggle against a secret conviction that she was not valued as a colleague. She could scarcely stop smiling for the rest of the day, though it was one of the busiest she had known on Pantomime.

Despite her pleasure in her clearly much improved professional relationship with Charles Patrick, Kate was still downright glad when her shift finished. Her back ached and she knew she would find it difficult to stop thinking about the patients even after she left the hospital. Normally she would have enjoyed a relaxing evening with Nell and the dogs, but Nell was off to a party with Richard, the dogs had been stolen, and, although it was tempting to imagine that Charles might come down and chat to her if she started gardening, she really did not feel in the mood for more hard physical labour.

In the changing-room Kate put on a cool cotton top and jeans and wondered what she should do. A swim, perhaps? But solitary swimming was not much fun. A meal out? The same thing applied. She could go and see a film but the cinema would be hot and dark—she really wanted to be in the open air on such an evening, yet somehow she did not relish returning alone to the empty flat.

I know, I'll get some chips and walk along the prom eating them, like any other holidaymaker, Kate decided. It'll do me good to relax, because back in the flat it'll be dull alone, and I'll start thinking about Stevie and Carl and baby Eagles, and that's no way to prepare myself for whatever tomorrow has in store.

And, once on the promenade, she was sure she had made the right decision. Everyone was in a good mood—people crowded the wide paving, children shouted and ran, adults laughed and teased one another. Kate got her fish and chips, then walked along to the small theatre. The show had changed the previous weekend and now crowds were queueing up to go in, lots of children among them, so Kate strolled over to look at the photographs of the artistes exhibited outside.

The main attraction seemed to be a young man who had once presented children's television programmes and a girl who still read the regional news. Smiling to herself at the oddness of human behaviour—for why should two such diverse people attract such crowds to come and watch them trying to act in a light-hearted comedy?—Kate moved away from the theatre. No doubt the kids in the queue would thoroughly enjoy seeing someone whose face they knew from the telly, even if they were disappointed to realise that the stars were just ordinary people, after all.

I wonder what the show will be like? Kate mused as she walked. Perhaps I might book for later in the week.

She was halfway across the road, almost back on the main part of the promenade, when a most peculiar sound came from behind her, a sort of *whump*, followed by a long, sustained roar.

Kate turned and stared, and saw the theatre suddenly enveloped in a cloud of smoke. Very slowly, it seemed, the building was collapsing on one knee while great chunks of masonry fell and clouds of dust rose in the air. The noise seemed continuous and it was accompanied, now, by shrieks and screams, a whistle blowing violently, the sound of skidding tyres as vehicles tried to stop, to swerve, and the hiss of air brakes and the screech of a long skid as each driver reacted in his own way to the sudden explosion.

Kate set off at a run across the road. She dodged stationary vehicles and ran in front of moving ones. All she could think of was the children, dozens of children, happily queueing to see a show. . .and then this!

Already a good many people were milling around. Kate leapt for a phone box. . .the phone was dead. She ran out, and collided with a figure she knew—Dr Ahmed, from the ENT Department.

'Oh, doctor, this phone's out of order. . .can someone phone for an ambulance?'

'We'll need a dozen, and a whole team of helpers,' the young doctor said grimly. 'I'll see to that, Nurse—you go and do what you can.'

Kate ran back to the theatre, or rather the ruins of the theatre. People were trying to move the wreckage with their bare hands, crying that the child in front of them. . .the woman. . .an old friend. . .had been just here, just here, when the explosion happened.

'I'm a nurse,' Kate told an elderly man who seemed to be trying to get the would-be rescuers into some sort of team to begin to move the rubble. 'What can I do?'

'See to anyone they bring out. . .there's a woman over there—she's in a bad way; she left her two children with an aunt who was taking them to see the show. . .see to her, would you?'

Kate went obediently over to the pale-faced woman. She was clearly very pregnant and she had a small boy by the hand. 'Philip ran back to ask me for money for icecreams,' she said in a low, dazed voice. 'But Tessa stayed with my sister Jenny. . .they were right inside; they weren't even queueing any more; they're in there somewhere!'

The little boy clinging to her hand whimpered and pressed his face against his mother's dress.

'I'm frightened,' he said. 'Mum, where's our Tessa?'

Kate knelt on the ground and rumpled the little boy's hair.

'Tessa will soon be brought out; she'll be all right,' she said soothingly. 'Will you come over here and sit down and look after Mummy?'

The child would have obeyed but the mother, clutching her stomach, did not want to leave the scene. She clearly thought that if she was actually nearby it might help to rescue her daughter, and Kate did not feel she could over-persuade her.

'Nurse?' A young man Kate recognised as a taxi driver who had been one of the first on the scene caught hold of her arm. 'Ah, someone said you were a nurse. We've got a lad out. . .can you come?'

Kate nodded, then turned to the mother and child.

'See? We'll get Tessa soon. You stay here, but you must sit down, my dear, and wait,' she told the woman. 'It won't do anyone any good if you collapse, or start to have the baby right now.'

Having seen the expectant mother at least seated, she turned to the young man who had come for her.

'All right, let's go!'

Darkness fell, and still the rescuers laboured. Kate worked as hard as anyone. Medical teams arrived, the St John's Ambulance people and the Red Cross came, the fire service used their heavy equipment, and, one by one, survivors and, alas, those who had not been so lucky, were brought from the ruined building.

Tessa was brought out before dark, blackened, bruised and with both legs broken, but so glad to see her brother and mother unhurt that she cried for the first time since the accident. One little cousin was found nearby, crushed by the fallen masonry, but the family kept their grief from Tessa, who needed all the help and support they could give her, and Kate soldiered on, drank tea from a plastic cup, ate a ham roll and carried her syringes and makeshift slings and dressings wherever they were needed.

She was working on one of the actors, trying to stop the bleeding from a wound in his forehead, when she sat back for a moment, feeling light-headed and dizzy, and looked about her. The crowd had thinned now—the police were keeping idlers away—but a movement on the opposite side of the promenade caught her eye. A man was walking a dog over there, a large dog.

It was Clyde! Kate was suddenly certain it was Clyde. She stood up, half-turned towards the road, and then turned back. What a fool she was—as if it mattered that the dog had been stolen when there were children and adults who might die if she just abandoned her job!

'Over here, Nurse!'

One of the men moving the rubble with his bare hands, moving it so gently and carefully that she had already marvelled at his patience, was calling her.

'I'm coming,' Kate called back. She set off, and saw Nell, who had come with one of the emergency teams, taking a break for a drink and something to eat. 'Guess what? I've just seen Clyde!'

Nell smiled wanly. She was looking as weary as Kate now felt, for she and Richard had been at the ice-rink when the emergency call came over the loudspeakers, and she had been tired when she'd arrived.

'Then if he's still in the area you'll probably have a chance to ask his owner why he didn't knock on the door and ask for his dogs back,' she observed. 'That young girl died, Kate.'

'I'm sorry,' Kate said helplessly. 'We're all doing our best, but we can't win 'em all.'

Presently, she told herself, I'll have another break, just to give myself a chance. But, for now, let's see what they've found over there.

CHAPTER SEVEN

IT WOULD have been lovely to have said that she toiled on tirelessly, Kate thought to herself as the night passed, but in fact she was very tired indeed. Despite the fact that other nurses and doctors were arriving all the time, it never seemed the moment to slow down a little. Not with people still buried beneath the rubble. At various times she saw Nell and Richard, Hannah from Casualty and Dr Souter from Orthopaedics, but then one of the firemen would shout and she would forget everything but the job in hand.

At one point Bob Nettall appeared, coming over to see her as she helped to get a badly injured teenager on to a stretcher.

'Marvellous work you've been doing, Kate,' Bob said cheerfully. 'I told the boss you were down here, slogging away. He's been operating for hours—you'll find Pantomime crammed to the eyebrows tomorrow, as well as the rest of the hospital. I wonder why there were so many kids, though?'

'Children's matinée,' Kate said briefly. She was setting up a drip by the teenager who was just about to be loaded into the ambulance. 'Are the injuries very bad, Bob? Are there many fatalities?'

'It's difficult to generalise,' Bob told her. 'Some are really bad, as you must know, but others look a lot worse than they are. A great deal of blood comes from quite a slight scalp wound, and quite often we've had someone in who's only got broken bones from the falling masonry. But look, isn't it about time you had a break? Dr Ahmed was saying you were one of the first on the scene. What were you doing down here, anyway?'

'Just passing,' Kate said ruefully, checking the cannula and then standing back so that the ambulancemen could take over. 'As for a break, I think I've got beyond that. I shall just keep going until I drop, I think. And someone who lives near by has sent out sandwiches and hot coffee, which has been a marvellous help. It makes you rest for a moment, and after that you feel you could go on forever.'

'Well, you can't; you're only human, and it won't do to work until you drop,' Dr Nettall said reprovingly. 'But if you ask me it won't be long before everyone's out. Those men are working like Trojans. Oh, and Adèle Fox is back on the ward—came in to give what help she could. And Estelle's working in Casualty, believe it or not, actually consenting to being ordered around and getting her hands dirty. Perhaps there's some good in her after all.'

'Oh, I'm sure there is,' Kate agreed as the ambulancemen began to edge the stretcher into their vehicle. She followed, the infusion set held high and steady, speaking over her shoulder to Bob. 'Perhaps it needed something like this to bring out the doctor in her, so to speak.'

'Yes, you're probably right. Plus the fact that Charles popped in and saw her working, and said that, in his opinion, some people are better with adults and some with kids, and Estelle's better with adults.' Bob took the infusion set from Kate and climbed up into the ambulance, then sat down at the head of the stretcher, steadying the drip. 'She's not so inclined to assume an adult is in her power, and she gives some thought to adults' feelings. For some reason she doesn't think of kids as being quite human!'

'It's probably because she's never had a child of her own,' Kate agreed as the ambulance drew away from the kerb. 'See you later, Bob!'

'Sure you will. . .and don't forget what I said. Let someone else take over before you're worn out!'

Kate smiled but did not reply. There was no point. So long as there were injured being brought out of the wreckage, so long as she was needed, she would stay here and do her best. That was what being a nurse was all about—no, she corrected herself, that was what being a *human being* was all about. She was lucky, she had the expertise, but others who had worked here uncomplainingly all night were simply doing their best for their fellow men, and obeying orders.

'Kate!'

It was one of the cadet nurses, waving wildly. Sue, a pleasure-loving little blonde with rosy cheeks and a penchant for very short skirts. Kate hurried over to her. She had always liked the younger girl but had never believed she would stick to nursing because Sue was too full of fun and too easygoing for all the studying and hard work which lay before her. Now, however, Kate's respect for the teenager had increased tenfold. Sue had arrived in a party dress and high heels; she had borrowed an old pair of plimsolls, had tied back her fluffy yellow curls with an old shoelace, and had been rooting through the rubble now for hours and hours. Her party dress was filthy, her skin was covered in the dust which arose every time masonry was shifted, and her nails were broken right down to the quicks. But her eyes shone brightly in her dirty face and her enthusiasm and energy had not flagged all night long.

'Kate, look at this!'

Kate hurried over to Sue, who held a bundle in her arms. It must be property which someone had left with her—it was too small to be a child. Kate looked down into the dirty, dusty bundle, and it was a baby, a really tiny child of only a few weeks. . .and even as she began to smile, looking down into the small face, Sue gave a gasp of horror and almost thrust the baby at Kate.

'Look, it's stopped breathing. . .Oh, Kate, it's going blue! What shall we do?'

Kate did not have to think. She snatched the small, bruised and battered body from the younger girl, her mind racing. Such a tiny creature, but resuscitation for babies was not so very different from the method used for adults.

She laid the baby on the paving and knelt beside it, moving the small jaw gently upwards, her fingers searching for the brachial pulse in the child's upper arm. She thought she could just feel a movement, but with her other hand she was opening the baby's mouth, checking that there was no obvious obstruction which might have have caused the little creature to choke or hold its breath. She dared not use the blind finger-sweep as she would have done for an adult or an older child in case she inadvertently pushed dirt or some other object further down the child's throat. However, her finger found nothing; the airway seemed clear.

Right. Mouth-to-mouth resuscitation, sealing the nose with her own cheek, while gently manipulating the chest with two fingers, having judged where the baby's nipple area was so that she could start compressing a finger's width below.

She was lucky; half a dozen carefully controlled breaths and the small diaphragm suddenly jerked once, then again, and then she felt the dilation which meant that the child was breathing unassisted once more.

Kate moved back and Sue, kneeling opposite her, reached out a gentle finger and touched the baby's filthy and bloodstained cheek.

'Is. . .is it all right? Oh, Kate, is it. . .is it. . .?'

'She's breathing steadily,' Kate said, her voice a trifle shaky. She stood up, the child in her arms. 'She's got a cut on her poor little head and she's bruised all over, but hopefully, she should be all right now. Oh, look, pink bootees. . .She really is a girl!'

Why this innocent observation should have had the effect it did neither girl could have said, but Sue glanced down at the tiny feet and burst into tears, and Kate, holding the child as if she were the most precious object in the universe, promptly followed suit. The two of them stood there, tears running down their dirty faces, and then the baby gave a little mutter and turned her head into Kate's front, clearly seeking sustenance.

'Oh, dear,' Kate said, wiping the tears away as best she could with the back of one hand and doubtless spreading the dirt everywhere. 'Poor little soul, she's hungry! She must be all right if she's hungry. Oh, Sue, I'm so happy!'

'She's awfully bruised and dirty,' Sue sniffed,

stroking the wisps of hair away from the baby's small face. 'She'd better go with the next ambulance, hadn't she?'

'Yes, definitely. I never asked, but where did your find her? And was there an adult anywhere near?'

'Not so far as I know, but they're still digging, of course. Oh, look, there's an ambulance drawing up; if we hurry we can get her aboard that one.'

The two girls hurried over to the kerbside, but to her own secret surprise Kate absolutely refused to let go of the baby when the ambulance attendant tried to relieve her of her precious burden.

'No, not this one,' she said firmly. 'I'm going to see her on to the ward myself. Another couple of minutes and she could have been dead. I'm not taking any more chances with little pinky-boots.'

Sue laughed at the nickname, waved, and then turned back to the theatre once more, and Kate squeezed into a corner with the baby securely held in her arms and endured the swift but horribly uncomfortable journey, emerging breathlessly into Casualty with her small charge.

While the baby was X-rayed Kate took the opportunity to have a good clean up and to put on a uniform, though she kept her dirty things handy so that she could change back before returning to the theatre.

'The baby's lucky—just a couple of broken ribs, and a lot of bruising,' they told her in X-ray. 'What name shall we put on the plates?'

But here Kate was unable to help, merely recommending that they ask everyone who came through their hands whether they knew anything about a baby girl, aged around eight to ten weeks, who had been in the theatre that day.

'No plaster for you,' Dr Saul said after he'd examined the X-rays. 'A nice warm bath is the best medicine, Staff, and then a feed and bed. Keep her warm and quiet and she'll do very well.'

'I'll do that,' Kate said, and carried Pinky up to the ward.

Adèle Fox, bustling around, greeted her with relief and her small charge with delight.

'A baby! Oh, Kate, it's good to see you; I'm giving Sister Buxton a hand but she could do with every member of staff she can get—can you see to that baby?'

'I can, and I will,' Kate said cheerfully. 'One bath, one feed, and then one sleepy girl will probably snore the clock round.'

'Who—you or the baby?' Adèle said, chuckling at her own wit. 'Off you go, then. And when you've done you should go home, you know; get some sleep.'

Kate smiled, but organised the bath, then the feed, and was sitting with Pinky in the crook of her arm, watching the child's mouth work rhythmically, her fingers curling and uncurling, while the milk-level in the bottle fell steadily, when the door of the cubicle she had chosen opened.

She could have glanced over her shoulder, but she did not need to do so; a hand touching her shoulder was sufficient. It was Charles Patrick standing there; she knew it as certainly as she knew her own name. However, she glanced up, a smile tilting her mouth.

'Well, Kate? Getting fond of baby Hunter? Her mother's just had an emergency operation but she should be all right, so I'm told. It was bright of you to alert the staff in Casualty—they found the mother quite soon after the baby had left them. She came in with some nasty injuries, so they prepped her for Theatre at once and just before she was anaesthetised she mumbled something about her baby daughter, so they were able to reassure her.'

'Poor dear—but at least the baby's safe. You don't know her name, do you, sir? I've been calling her Pinky.'

Mr Patrick had moved round so that they could talk more easily. He shook his head at her words, however.

'No, I'm afraid not. Pinky will have to do for now. And I gather from the staff that when Mrs Hunter does come round she'll have a lot to thank you for. I understand the child had stopped breathing?'

'Yes. But she started again very quickly once I'd taken steps,' Kate said, stroking the baby's clean, soft cheek. 'I don't imagine she actually stopped for more than a minute or two, but it's just occurred to me—is it possible that brain damage could have resulted in that short time?'

'It's possible—but, judging from the way the little one is taking her milk, and from her hand movements and the way her eyes followed me when I moved just now, I should say you caught her in time. She's a lucky little girl, is baby Hunter.'

'That's a great weight off my mind,' Kate admitted. 'One thing, though, Mr Patrick: what was Mrs Hunter doing at the theatre with such a young child?'

'She had been looking after her nephew, who's seven, and had arranged with her sister to take the little boy down to the theatre to see the show. Apparently he was going with a group of children. Anyway, she'd left him with his friends and was about to go when she remembered she hadn't left him any money for an icecream in the interval. She'd just got inside the building when the bomb went off. She told the ambulancemen that much, but unfortunately they weren't the ones who brought you and baby Hunter back, so they weren't able to reassure her.'

'Then it's as well the people in Casualty told her,' Kate said as the last of the milk was drained from the bottle. She sat the baby up and was about to swing her on to her shoulder when she remembered the ribs, so kept the small figure upright, on her knee.

'Some damage, eh?' Mr Patrick said. 'Ribs?'

'That's right. It won't be possible to burp her on your shoulder for a bit—good thing we've all had practice with baby Potter and her hiatus hernia!'

She began to rub the small nightgowned back, but Mr Patrick took the baby neatly from her and sat down with her on his own knee, beginning to bring up her wind in a highly professional manner.

'You lean back while I do this,' he advised. 'You look exhausted, Kate.'

'I am tired,' Kate owned, leaning back in her chair and closing her eyes for a moment. 'What happened to the nephew?'

'Badly shocked, and a broken collarbone, but he's been taken home by his parents. Mrs Hunter will be all right; Mr Troughton had to operate to sort her out, but I don't think her injuries were life-threatening. They're a lucky little family.'

As he spoke he moved the baby slightly so that Kate could look into her small face. The eyes were sleepy slits, the cheeks rosy with food and warmth. 'I'd say someone here was just about ready for a good night's rest. Which is her cot?'

'That one. The other is full of baby Sharon Crane. Shall I. . .?'

'No need.' The surgeon laid the baby carefully down, head turned to one side, smoothing the disposable sheet flat beneath the small cheek. Kate bent over the cot, critically regarding her charge.

'Yes, you've done that very professionally,' she said. 'Thanks for your help, Mr Patrick.' She straightened and turned towards the door. 'And now it's once more unto the breach, dear friends.'

'No, Kate. Not back to the promenade,' Charles Patrick said quickly. 'You've done more than your share tonight.'

'Haven't we all?' Kate turned and left the cubicle, the surgeon close at her heels. 'I'll hitch a lift in the next ambulance and do my bit for a while yet. I'm not too tired to be useful.'

The surgeon followed her down to Reception, still arguing, but once there he was immediately hauled off to Theatre once more and Kate was able to make her escape. She put her uniform back rather regretfully and dressed once again in her dusty jeans, but at least, she comforted herself, her person was clean again, if not for long!

When she got out of the ambulance outside the theatre she was glad she had come. For a moment she saw the scene as if it were a stage set—tiny figures toiling to move the rubble by

the light of the arc-lamps set up by the firemen
and the police, soldiers from the nearby barracks
struggling with chunks of masonry, ambulance
staff handling the injured with infinite gentle-
ness, nurses in uniform and in civvies rendering
first-aid, giving injections, taking orders from
weary doctors whose clothing was as filthy as
that of the humblest rescue-worker. It looked
exciting and romantic for a moment, and then
Kate stepped down on to the broad stretch of
paving and she was no longer an observer but a
part of what was happening.

'Oh, Nurse, can you come here a moment?
It's only a dog but it's hurt. . .can you tell if it's
leg is broken or what?

Her visit to the hospital had given her a new
lease of life, Kate thought gratefully. She hurried
over to the soldier who had called her, to do
what she could for the scruffy little mongrel
dog.

'Kate, come on, I'm driving you home. Don't
shake your head at me, because I'm not asking,
I'm telling. You've done your share and more;
now it's time you let someone else have a go.'

Kate looked up. Charles Patrick loomed over
her. He was in shirtsleeves, he had a bristly chin
and his eyes were deeply shadowed, but he
smiled as her eyes met his.

'You think I look a mess? You should see

yourself, young woman! Are you going to get into the car or am I going to have to carry you?'

'I'm tempted to let you carry me,' Kate confessed, walking along beside him. 'Gracious, is that dawn in the sky over there?'

'It is. Well, it'll be sunrise before you get home, actually, since dawn broke a while ago. It's going to be a nice day, weather-wise, though I imagine that our workload now beggars description.' He helped her into the passenger-seat, then went round and got behind the wheel. 'I'd like to lay hands on the louts who planted that bomb,' he added through clenched teeth. 'Women and children always go to the early show and those bastards knew it when they planted the bomb.'

'Bomb? Then it really was a bomb?'

'That's right. Some terrorist organisation probably, trying to make a point with the lives of the innocent. Did you realise why there were so many kids in the queue? Apparently a local organisation invited a number of children from the local army camp to see the show, and I suppose people with the sort of mind which wants to kill soldiers aren't too fussy if they end up killing soldiers' wives and kiddies as well. Oh, Kate, sometimes I wonder about the human race and why we try to hard to preserve it.'

'So do I,' Kate admitted in a low voice. 'So do I, Charles.'

They drove for a while in silence. The sky was

brightening now with every moment; colours were creeping back on to the land. Charles sighed and leaned forward to switch on the radio.

'Better hear what the newscasters have to say about it all,' he remarked. 'Perhaps they'll catch the swines.'

'Mm. . .only they never seem to, do they?' Kate said sadly. 'There are no clues to follow up when you set a trap to catch anyone at all, no connections, no bits of information which will prove who did it.'

'This may be the exception,' Charles said hopefully. 'Ah, just in time; we'll catch the local headlines.'

The two sat and listened bitterly while the newscaster told them that a terrorist group had already claimed responsibility for the outrage in Colney Bay,

'How they can boast. . .? All those kiddies,' Kate said despairingly. 'Not even an apology for no warning being given. . .they aren't men, are they, Charles? They're animals.'

'Calling them animals does a disservice to the animal kingdom,' Charles observed. 'They behave in a way no self-respecting animal would. Now we're home, and you're going straight to bed.'

She was so tired that the swayed in her seat and made no demur when he all but lifted her out of it and took her not just to her back door but right into the flat. He stood in the kitchen for a moment, then said. 'No time to waste on niceties such as washing. . .want me to make you a hot drink while you climb into bed?'

'No, thanks. I just want to sleep,' Kate mumbled. He came with her into the bedroom, knelt and took her sandals off, sat her on the covers while he removed her borrowed sweater, for the night had grown colder as darkness had advanced, and then she smiled sleepily up at him as he rolled her between the covers.

'You are good!' Kate muttered, her voice slurring with sleep. 'You're so tired, too. . .just as tired as me. Go to bed, won't you?'

He laughed softly, tucking her in.

'I will. I was supposed to take the first train from Colney Bay station tomorrow, at six o'clock, to go up to London for a conference, but in the circumstances I think I'll give it a miss. Besides, there's something I want to talk to you about.'

'Mm-hmm,' Kate droned into her pillow. 'What was that?'

'Well, you remember when you leapt into my arms in the garden that night, and accused me of following you, that I said I'd been to the theatre?'

Sleep, abruptly deserted Kate. She remembered all too well. She sat up on her elbow.

'I remember. You went with Estelle.'

Charles laughed softly but put out a hand and

pushed her gently back on to her pillow. 'No. Wrong. I went with Mr Barlowe and his wife, but I could scarcely tell you to go to the ENT specialist for confirmation of my whereabouts, and since I saw Estelle in the audience, and exchanged a few words with her during the interval. . .well, it seemed like a good idea at the time for you to check with her.'

'I see,' Kate said, trying not to smile. 'Oh, so you didn't take her to the theatre, then?'

'No, I didn't. I've never been even slightly interested in Estelle; my senior staff nurse interested me *far* more.'

'Oh, sure,' Kate murmured. 'See you in the morning, then, Mr Patrick.'

'There's a forfeit for that. . .' He loomed over the bed, then drew back, shaking his head, smiling down at her.

'No, not fair; you're far too tired to tease. Sleep well, darling Katie.'

Darling Katie? I imagined it, decided Kate, and dived into slumber as an eager child dived into a swimming-pool.

Kate woke two hours later without the slightest idea what had roused her. She only knew she was wide awake and her brain was ticking over at an alarming rate of knots. She lay still for a moment, wondering why on earth she should suddenly feel so lively, as though while she had slept she had found the solution to all the world's problems. Then she remembered the explosion, and the terrible consequences, the dead and injured, the bereaved.

She frowned up at the ceiling, where sunshine danced, then glanced at her alarm clock. It was early still, not yet six. She had been dreaming; she had dreamed that she was walking along the promenade with Bonnie and Clyde and a man had come up to her and she had known at once. . .

What had she known? Dreams were so strange and confusing, yet sometimes they seemed to discover a truth which the dreamer had not, waking, known. Kate lay on her back gazing up at the flickering shadow-pictures on the ceiling and straining her memory. It was something to do with the theft of the dogs, something on the radio. . .

When recollection came it hit her like a thunderclap. What had Charles called the dogs' owners? Mick and Pat, with Pat standing, in this instance, for Patricia. Which meant that they were almost certainly Irish. And Irish terrorists had claimed responsibility for planting the bomb. And, dammit, she had *seen* with her own eyes a man walking along the promenade, glancing over towards the theatre, when the rescue work was at its height! She was suddenly sure, with the sort of certainty which could not be denied, that the dog-walker had been the man who had planted the bomb. After all, what better cover could there be for suspicious behaviour than a dog? The man could have had the bomb in a haversack; he and the dog could have been strolling past the theatre—it would have been a simple matter to have gone into the foyer to push the bomb out of sight behind a plant or a seat. And if he had been unlucky, if someone had approached him, he could just have said that he was wanting to book seats for the show but did not like to go over to the ticket office with the dog.

By now Kate was sitting bolt upright in bed, her mind racing. She should go to the police—but they would laugh at her, tell her she was imagining the whole affair. Unless she moved fast, the man, and the two dogs, would be far away anyway. Who had said something about the first train to London? Or would they go in the opposite direction, try to get aboard a boat-train for Ireland? She supposed they would have to abandon the dogs again in that case, though, and she guessed that all ports would be watched. It would be London, she was sure of it. The man and the woman who had perpetrated the outrage would be at the station right now, preparing to get on the six o'clock train for London! It would have to be by public transport if she was right about Maria's former tenants being the bombers; she remembered Charles's saying that the dogs' reaction to the car was one of novelty, since neither Mick nor Pat owned or drove a vehicle.

Kate leaped out of bed. She rushed over to her chest of drawers, abstracted jeans and a T-shirt and pulled them on. Washing would have to wait. . .she must get to the station without a moment's delay!

In the hall she saw the telephone and grabbed it. She phoned the police, and the desk-sergeant, his voice suddenly waking up as she told of her suspicions, agreed to get someone to the station at once.

'He'll have two red setters with him, and probably a woman,' Kate said excitedly. 'The dogs know me; I'll be there.'

She rang off while the policeman was still telling her to leave it to them, and ran out of the house. In the stable, right next door to Charles's beautiful car, was a bicycle, old and shabby, which Maria sometimes rode down to the shops. Kate hurled herself on to the saddle and pedalled briskly down the drive. She had been tempted to try to wake Charles Patrick, but it really wasn't fair and anyway he might have woken already and gone. If he was at the station. . .but she had said nothing of her suspicions the previous night because then she had had no suspicions. No, this was her idea and she was the only person who could do anything about it.

By some frantic pedalling Kate reached the

station at ten to six. She could see no policemen, but they were unlikely to be visible, she realised. There were a surprising number of people waiting for the train, though, but no dogs. Not one.

Kate's heart sank. It was all a wild-goose chase; she had been too clever; the dog-thieves could not have had anything to do with the bombing, or if they had they were too bright to make for the station. She must have been mad, thinking they would do something so obvious!

The train came in noisily and porters began hurling newspapers down from the guard's van. The guard's van! They were loading it up on the far end of the platform and, now that she came to think of it, two dogs would scarcely travel in the ordinary compartments of a crowded train with their owners. They would be fastened up in the guard's van for their owners to collect on arrival at their destination!

Kate set off at a run along the platform. And she was right! There they were, Bonnie and Clyde, with a dark-haired woman bending over them, checking that their leads were correctly fastened. Kate went to go towards her, then looked wildly round. There was that man Mick, too; he could not be far away. . .and where on earth were the police? A tall man with a newspaper, clad in a navy mackintosh, was strolling down the platform towards her. . .could he be a CID man in plain clothes?

Kate turned and hurried towards him. She stopped in front of him and tugged at his sleeve.

'The dogs are in the guard's van,' she hissed. 'The woman's with them, but I can't see. . .'

The man stared at her for a second and then caught her by the shoulders and literally threw her down. Kate felt the platform crash across her shoulders, saw the train itself getting closer to her, and knew that she would fall between carriage and platform, knew she would be killed. . .knew, as she heard the man swearing beneath his breath, that she had been a gullible fool. It had been the bomber himself she had approached; she had ruined the whole thing and she would die for it!

She was screaming, trying to stop herself rolling under the train, when something incredibly hard and heavy smote her across the head and she lost consciousness.

Charles Patrick drove on to the station forecourt and stopped with a screech of brakes at an angle to the entrance. He was out of the car and running before the car had come to a halt, fear for Kate almost depriving him of breath. She had come down here to tackle the terrorists, he knew it, and his main memory of Mick was of the innate coldness of the man. The other would not hesitate to kill Kate if she got in his way. . .Where on earth was she?

He ran across the foyer and through the

gateway on to the platform. Immediately he saw her approaching a tall man in a mac, who was carrying a newspaper in one hand. For a split-second he hesitated. . .then recognition came and sheer, blind terror sent him across the intervening space like a bullet.

She'd be killed! She was the pluckiest, cheek-iest, most irritating girl he knew—and he loved her! But had he told her so? Oh, no, nothing but hints and half-truths, in case she proved her independence by turning him down, proving to the mighty Charles Patrick that she meant what she said—she really did intend to be a career nurse!

He was within a few feet of the couple when the man suddenly swung out viciously, knock-ing Kate to the ground and then giving her a hefty kick, rolling her towards the train which had actually started, was actually moving!

In a blur of rage Charles crossed the last couple of feet and grabbed Kate, then, without hesitating, he swung with all his strength at her attacker. The man's square, aggressive chin took the full force of the blow and he went down on his back with a sickening thud. From the train someone screamed, people converged on them, but Charles was indifferent.

He was on his knees, scooping Kate's warm and breathing body into the safety of his arms.

CHAPTER EIGHT

IT WAS always a weird experience to regain consciousness, but to awaken to find oneself in strange surroundings was, in addition, extremely frightening. Kate saw first handsome striped wallpaper, then white paintwork, then the curve of a white cotton pillowslip. Her eyelids were extremely heavy, though, and it was quite an effort to look further. I'm in bed, she thought drowsily. What happened after the explosion? I wasn't hurt, though I ache dreadfully, as though I'd been run over by a. . .

On the thought she remembered. The bombers, the dogs, the train! Her heart began to beat to a fast staccato rhythm, like train-wheels speeding over the rails, clickety-click, clickety-click! She had seen the dogs in the guard's van, had tried to tell a policeman, only he wasn't a policeman at all, he was one of the bombers and he had knocked her down and then kicked her viciously towards the train!

So this was a hospital? Kate opened her eyes again and peered about her, actually moving her aching head on the pillow. Heavy velvet curtains, partly pulled, with some sort of blind diffusing the sunshine so that it seemed hazy and remote. Where had she seen that type of blind before? And those velvet curtains in a light biscuit colour? She was moving her head back again with care, taking in a built-in wardrobe, a dressing-table and a chair with a striped satin seat when she saw a movement out of the corner of her eye.

A tall stranger was approaching the bed! Without meaning to, Kate winced away, then gathered her courage and looked again. There were two men, not one, and the second was a familiar tall figure. . .of course, that was why she had recognised the curtains—she had seen them from the outside. . .this was Charles Patrick's flat!

'Katie? Are you awake? This is Detective-Sergeant Dixon wanting a word.'

Kate smiled uncertainly up at the two men who now stood by the bed, looking down at her.

'Oh. . .hello,' she said feebly. 'What on earth am I doing here? I thought I went under the train.'

Both men smiled but Charles's lips had a rueful twist.

'My love, for one terrible moment I thought the same. I've never moved so fast in my life! I crossed the platform on wings, I swear it, and scooped you up just before you disappeared.'

'Oh. Well, thanks,' Kate said vaguely. Had he

called her his love? She was still dreaming, clearly! 'I ache all over.'

'You're black and blue from top to toe,' the surgeon admitted. 'You're a heroine, though— the police stopped the train and arrested the man and woman with the two dogs.'

'How did they recognise them?' Kate demanded, trying to frown and hastily stopping. It hurt too much. 'The woman was with the dogs, but the man. . .'

'Well, we didn't think an innocent man would throw you down on to the platform just because you approached him and then try to roll you towards the train,' Charles said, grinning. 'And I was able to identify him as the owner of the two red setters in the guard's van because as soon as I saw him I knew him as Maria's former tenant.'

'Yes, of course. I forgot you knew him,' Kate admitted. 'But how did you get there, Charles?'

'The police sergeant tried to ring you back after you put the phone down on him. I was prowling round and heard your telephone ringing so I went in and answered it. You were in such a rush that you didn't lock the door, fortunately. As soon as he told me what you'd said I got into the car and came straight to the station. Just in time to see you walk slap-bang up to Mick. My darling girl, whatever possessed you to do such a dangerous thing?'

'I thought he was a plain-clothes policeman,'

Kate said resentfully. 'He looked just like one.'
She glanced up at the detective sergeant, who
was wearing a brown jacket and blue jeans.
'Well. . .he looked the way I thought a plain
clothes cop would look,' she amended.

'It's a popular misconception, Miss Reagan,'
the policeman said, smiling down at her. 'And
now do you think you could answer some of my
questions? I'm sure you've still got plenty of
your own to ask, but if you could spare me a
few minutes. . .'

'Yes, of course,' Kate said, though she still
ached dreadfully and her head was thumping.
'I'd love a drink, though. My mouth feels like
the bottom of a parrot cage.'

'I'll get you a nice cup of tea,' Charles said.
'Shan't be a moment, Sergeant.'

'Oh. . . I'd rather you stayed. . .' Kate was
beginning, then stopped herself. She was being
very foolish. . .and no one had answered her
question as to what she was doing in Mr
Patrick's flat. She tried to heave herself further
up the bed and succeeded, then addressed the
young policeman.

'This is Mr Patrick's flat, of course, but just
why am I in bed here, instead of in my own
place?'

The policeman smiled, then shrugged.

'I dare say he brought you here because he
wanted to be able to keep an eye on you, Miss
Reagan. He said something about the hospital

being packed out after the terrorist attack last night. But don't worry, I'm sure he isn't intending to kidnap you, especially as he was telling me you're planning a short engagement.'

Curiouser and curioser, as Alice in Wonderland would have said! A short engagement? Either she was going mad or the sergeant had got his wires crossed. And as for kidnapping. . .

'Oh, no. . .isn't. . .it wasn't. . . I didn't mean. . .' Kate stammered. 'I've got the downstairs flat, you see, but I dare say it was more sensible to being me up here. I dare say my flatmate's in no state to take care of me. . .not that I need taking care of, not now; I'm fine.'

It sounded feeble even to her own ears and she did not altogether blame the sergeant for the disbelieving look which he tried so hard to banish.

'You'll be right as rain given a night's sleep, I expect. Now do you want to tell me your full name, age, et cetera, and I'll fill them in on this form?'

'Sure,' Kate agreed. 'So long as I can remember them. I still feel rather dopey.'

She hoped that this would explain her strange inability to understand just why she was here. . .and then she glanced down, following the sergeant's eyes, and saw on the third finger of her small, practical left hand, a gold ring with a diamond and sapphire cluster which had certainly not been there earlier. She gave a gasp which she hastily turned into a cough. A short engagement! No wonder he had called her his love! Charles Patrick had pretended that he and she were engaged to be married—just let her get hold of her boss and he'd have some explaining to do!

'Well, I've seen the sergeant off and I've brought you a light lunch.' Charles came softly into the room, an uncertain smile hovering. Clearly, he was none too sure of his welcome. 'Feeling better, Katie?'

Kate propped herself up on her elbow and looked at the tray. Cold chicken and salad with new potatoes and butter, a tall glass of white wine and some crusty French bread. It would have been rather nice to have bidden him, in a faint voice, to take it away, but. . .she was awfully hungry and it looked awfully good!

'Yes, I'm feeling much better,' she said, letting him settle the tray comfortably across her knees. 'But you, Charles Patrick, have got some explaining to do. What's this ring doing on my finger and why did the sergeant think we were engaged?'

'Oh, dear! And I suppose you're wondering just what you're doing in my bed!'

Kate, briskly plying her knife and fork, nodded. Her mouth was too full for light conversation—for any conversation, come to that.

'Explain,' she commanded rather thickly.

'Oh. Right. From the beginning? From what happened on the platform right up to. . .to now?'

Nod, nod went Kate's head as her fork carried another load of salad to her mouth. Oh, she was hungry, and oh, it was delicious!

'Well, I brought you home after that dreadful explosion and saw you into bed and then went back to my own place and scrubbed up and boiled the kettle. I had intended to go back to the hospital, but there were plenty of doctors there and it occurred to me that you were exhausted and very vulnerable should anyone try to gain entry to the flat again. I was pretty sure you wouldn't have staggered out of bed and dropped the catch and of course I couldn't do it without staying at your place overnight. Well, I could have, but then I remembered Nell and so I left it.'

'It wouldn't have mattered; I think Nell must have spent the night. . .well, somewhere else,' Kate said, sipping her wine. 'I don't intend to enquire where because she was down at the theatre working her heart out, the same as we all were, but I did see Richard there too, and they've been getting on ever so much better lately, so I rather wonder if. . .'

'Considering where you are at this moment, you can scarcely accuse Nell of anything,' Charles said smoothly, then shook his head as

Kate scowled at him. 'It was only a joke, Katie, and in very poor taste, I dare say.'

'Yes, it was,' Kate said severely, trying not to laugh. 'But don't let me side-track you. What were you doing when I was running out of my flat and bicycling frantically down to the station? If I'd known you were awake and around I'd have knocked on your door and begged a lift!'

'I was in my kitchen, making myself a pot of tea and wondering whether you were awake as well and if you'd like a cup,' Charles admitted gloomily. 'When you think that for the whole of the rest of the night I'd patrolled round and round the building, just in case you might wake up and come to your window, or have a nightmare and scream, it was appallingly bad luck that when you did emerge—and did need help—I was probably bending over, getting the milk out of the fridge!'

'Oh, well, it was all right in the end,' Kate pointed out. 'But why on earth were you patrolling round? I mean if I'd had a nightmare what would you have done? You could scarcely rush in and wake me up!'

'I don't know. The fact is, Katie, I was hoping you'd emerge so I could pluck up my courage to tell you. . .to tell you. . .'

'Yes? Tell me what?'

'To tell you how I felt when I walked into that cubicle and saw you nursing baby Hunter. I had been told all about your prompt action by young

Susan Taylor and, of course, having checked out the little Hunter girl and having seen Mrs Hunter when she came in, crying out for her baby, all I should have felt, when I saw you, was relief that the baby was alive and well. And Katie, I was glad the baby was safe, but my main feeling was. . .well, I just thanked God that *you* were all right, and near me, and not in love with Bob Nettall. . .'

'How do you know I'm not in love with Bob?' Kate said crossly. 'He's a very nice guy.'

'Oh, sure. But you aren't, are you?'

'Well. . .no,' Kate admitted grudgingly, after a pause. 'So you wanted to tell me you were glad I'd managed to save Baby Hunter and——'

'No, dammit! I wanted to tell you that you meant a lot to me, and that I'd ever felt quite this way about a woman before, and I wanted to tell you how I. . .how I felt!'

'Well, that's very nice,' Kate said, gratified, though still a trifle puzzled. Her boss had never struck her as lacking confidence, yet here he was, all but stammering over a simple explanation! 'So you missed my cycling off by sheer bad luck, but heard the telephone ringing and, when I didn't answer, tried the back door and got in. What did the sergeant tell you?'

Charles groaned.

'That you were too headstrong, and had rushed to the station to confront the suspected terrorists. I knew what might easily happen and

I hurled myself into the car and tore after you, but of course you were on the bike so you cut through the pathway, which shortens the journey by a good half-mile, so you were probably two or three minutes ahead of me when you reached the station.'

'Yes, and I put my foot right in it by thinking the bomber was a cop, and he whacked me over the head and tried to push me under the train, and then. . .?' Kate was looking up at Charles as she spoke and saw the uncontrollable tremor which shook his frame at her words. 'You saved my life, Charles,' she said, rather timidly for her. 'I really am grateful.'

'Well. Anyway. So I clouted the fellow on the jaw and laid him out, and then I checked you over at the hospital and decided to bring you back here, partly because I could keep an eye on you better in my own place, but also because every bed in the hospital is full and I knew you wouldn't fancy waking up thirty or forty miles away in a strange hospital bed.'

'*You* checked me over?'

'Yes, indeed. I *am* a doctor, Kate.'

'So you are,' Kate said, knowing that her face was hot, which meant it would be pink, as well. 'And then you brought me back here, by ambulance, I suppose, but instead of leaving me in my flat you had me carried up here because the bed's bigger and you know the kitchen better and anyway, for all you knew, Nell might have been trying to sleep in our flat downstairs.'

'Yes, that's more or less how it was. And, of course, I did want to be able to keep in touch with the ward without running up your phone bill, if only to explain what had happened to my staff.'

'I hope you didn't go undermining my authority with the nursing staff by lurid tales of who was where,' Kate said, rather incoherently, the colour in her cheeks deepening, she was sure, from rose to beetroot. 'Oh, dear!'

'No, of course I didn't; I was very tactful. And now would you like some pudding, Staff Nurse Reagan?'

'Oh, is there a pudding? I've eaten an awful lot already, but perhaps I need lots of extra strength and things after my ordeal,' Kate said. 'Oddly enough, though, I do have a small pudding-shaped corner left despite all that lovely chicken and salad. . .what sort of pudding is it?'

'It isn't terrible exciting. Just vanilla ice-cream with chocolate sauce. And then coffee, of course.'

'That would be lovely,' Kate sighed, relinquishing her tray. 'But before you go could you just explain one more thing? While I was talking to that nice detective sergeant I noticed I was wearing a ring on the third finger of my left hand, and I'm positive I wasn't wearing it earlier.'

Now it was Charles who began to look a trifle hot and bothered.

'Ah. . .well, when the police rang to ask if you could make a statement it occurred to me that they might look at us a trifle askance. . . I believe I had said something about your being my fiancée, so I rang down to Maria and got her to lend me a dress-ring and. . .well, I more or less told the sergeant we were engaged.'

'I see. You wanted to save your reputation.'

'No, Kate, of course not! It was just. . .'

To her joy, Kate saw that Charles's lean cheeks were indeed slightly flushed. She smiled wickedly up at him, enjoying his discomfiture, and was about to tease him further when a thought occurred to her which took her mind completely off engagement rings. She was in her nightie!

'Charles, who undressed me and put on my nightie?'

The surgeon's face was a study. He was trying to look haughty and self-assured and instead was looking as guilty as a small boy caught rifling a sweet-shop.

'Umm. . .well, now. . .that's a fair question. . .how did you get undressed? I brought your nightie up from your flat, of course; I found it tucked under your pillow. And those jeans you were wearing were awfully tight—you couldn't possibly relax with them on. It was my considered medical opinion, Katie, my love, that you would be more comfortable in a nightie. And also,' he added irrepressibly, 'I guessed you'd look much prettier. And I was right.'

Kate's face was flaming.

'You took my clothes off? While I was unconscious?'

'If you'd been conscious you'd have done it yourself,' Charles pointed out righteously. 'Believe me, my darling girl, I didn't *want* to undress you, it was my duty.'

'And I'm not your darling girl,' Kate said crossly, tears coming to her eyes. 'You made up that engagement story to save your face! Why didn't you send for Nell to put me to bed?'

Charles Patrick sat down on the edge of the bed and took Kate's hot and embarrassed face between his hands.

'Kate, when I saw you on the platform, about to roll under that train, I knew I cared deeply for you—loved you, in fact. I'd have asked you to marry me then and there, but unfortunately you couldn't say yes because you were unconscious. And when you love a girl you want to take care of her yourself, not hand her over to some guy who won't give your girl the tender care she needs. So I told them you were my fiancée, checked you for broken bones or concussion, brought you back here and popped you into bed. And,' he added virtuously, 'I kept my eyes closed until the nightie was on and you were tucked up warmly.'

Between his hands, Kate's face trembled into laughter, though tears stood in her eyes.

'Oh, Charles, what a liar you are! You said I was black and blue!'

'Well, yes. Some bits of you are, but the rest, my adorable Kate, is pink and white and absolutely scrumptious, and will you kindly say you'll marry me and stop asking such bloody awkward questions?'

Kate looked up into his eyes and saw the seriousness underlying the laughter. She was beginning to smile, which made the tears spill over, but her smile faltered as his face drew nearer, as his mouth claimed hers.

It was a long kiss and somehow, when at last he moved away from her, Charles was lying on the bed and Kate was half out of the covers and pressed satisfyingly close.

'Oh, Charles,' Kate mumbled, her arms tightly round him as though she was afraid to let him go. 'Oh, Charles, I love you so much!'

'Not as much as I love you, Katie! Does that mean you'll marry me? Because if so, I shall probably hug you so hard that you'll have a completely fresh set of bruises to add to the existing ones.'

'Bruise away,' Kate whispered against his neck. 'Oh, hold me, Charles, hold me tight!'

Much later they lay side by side on top of the covers and talked over the past few weeks, clearing up mistakes and misunderstandings, laughing at each other and at themselves.

'I first realised I liked you more than I'd imagined when I saw you chatting away to young Nettall on the ward,' Charles admitted, a lazy arm looped about her shoulders. 'I've never thought of myself as the jealous type, but I had several twinges then, and the evening I came home to find Bob mowing the lawn and the pair of you looking so happy and easy with one another. . .' He actually ground his teeth and turned to look broodingly at Kate. 'How about you? You never showed the slightest sign of succumbing to my many and varied charms.'

'I was jealous of Estelle,' Kate admitted. 'You seemed to take her side, Charles, even when you must have known she was wrong. That made me cross, but it made me sure you had a weakness for her, too.'

'I didn't take her side so much as try to defend a young colleague,' Charles pointed out. 'But once I found out that she lied about her mistakes and was quite happy to see someone else blamed for them I began to be a bit more careful. Still, we despatched her to her next ward three weeks early, and I had several words with Mr Barlowe about her. I don't think she'll stay the course, actually. Apparently she's been talking about going into industry, where she'll do far less damage.'

'Good. It'll be lovely and peaceful on the ward without her.'

'Ye-es. But not for long, sweet Kate. You don't want to be a sister once we're married, do you?'

'Yes, I do,' Kate said indignantly. 'I'll leave when I start a family and not a moment before.'

'Oh, well, in *that* case we'll start a family at once. If not sooner. And we shouldn't just lie here enjoying ourselves, incidentally, because you haven't even seen the beautiful house I'm having built for us out on the point.'

'For us! You were having it built before you even met me!'

'True. But it was for you, even though I hadn't met you. It was for someone special, see?' He turned and kissed her on the eyebrow. 'You'll love it, but it's a long way from finished so you'll be able to have a say in all the decorating and the finishing touches.'

'If I weren't so comfortable perhaps I'd want to go and see it right now,' Kate murmured. 'Do you know, Charles, I can't believe all this—first that terrible bombing, and then all the excitement of actually catching the bombers, and now this!'

'Yes, it's pretty mind-blowing,' Charles agreed. 'You know that phone call I took a while back?'

'Yes; who was it? I never did ask.'

'It was the police. Apparently the fact is that the bomb wasn't supposed to go off when it did, but the fellow who planted it had Clyde with him, and the dog played up, kept messing about and started to bark, and the fellow thought he'd set the mechanism to go off in twenty-four hours, by which time they would have been well away, but he must have moved something which caused it to go off within a couple of hours of being planted. Terrible for the kids, but perhaps fewer were involved than if they had actually been inside the theatre.'

'Yes, it's true that the performance hadn't started,' Kate admitted. 'Good for Clyde. I know five fatalities seems a lot to us, but when you compare it with what might have happened had the theatre been full. . .We really ought to find out what's happening to Bonnie and Clyde, Charles, because they did nothing wrong, did they?'

'They did nothing wrong? What about my dahlia bed?'

Kate smothered a giggle, smoothing the side of his neck in a gesture both intimate and tender.

'Oh, that! Can we give them a good home, Charles? Do say we can. You love them as much as I do, admit it!'

'Oh, hell, so now I'm sharing you with a couple of dopey dogs as well as with a wardful of children! If you're absolutely set on it I suppose we shall have to have them, but, I warn you, it brings our starting a family even closer.'

'Oh, *thank* you, dearest Charles! Incidentally, shouldn't you be at work?'

'No. I was going to London to that conference, remember? Instead, I shall take care of you today, and tomorrow morning we'll go in together and tell everyone we're getting married.'

'And what about tonight? Are you going to repatriate me to the garden flat?'

'Kiss me!' Charles demanded, turning her face to his.

'In a moment. Are you taking me back to my own flat tonight?'

'Damn it, woman, are you never going to do as you're asked? Kiss me!'

It was clear she would never get an answer out of him until she had complied, so Kate closed her eyes, snuggled luxuriously close, and kissed him.

And somehow she forgot she'd not had an answer to her question!

From the author of Mirrors comes an enchanting romance

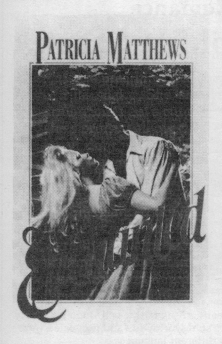

PATRICIA MATTHEWS

Caught in the steamy heat of America's New South, Rebecca Trenton finds herself torn between two brothers – she yearns for one, but a dark secret binds her to the other.

Off the coast of South Carolina lay Pirate's Bank – a small island as intriguing as the legendary family that lived there. As the mystery surrounding the island deepened, so Rebecca was drawn further into the family's dark secret – and only one man's love could save her from the treachery which now threatened her life.

W♥RLDWIDE

4 MEDICAL ROMANCES
AND 2 FREE GIFTS
From Mills & Boon

Capture all the excitement, intrigue and emotion of the busy medical world by accepting four FREE Medical Romances, plus a FREE cuddly teddy and special mystery gift. Then if you choose, go on to enjoy 4 more exciting Medical Romances every month! Send the coupon below at once to:

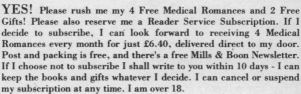

MILLS & BOON READER SERVICE, FREEPOST
PO BOX 236, CROYDON, SURREY CR9 9EL.

No stamp required

--- ✂ --- --- --- --- --- --- --- --- --- --- ✂ ---

YES! Please rush me my 4 Free Medical Romances and 2 Free Gifts! Please also reserve me a Reader Service Subscription. If I decide to subscribe, I can look forward to receiving 4 Medical Romances every month for just £6.40, delivered direct to my door. Post and packing is free, and there's a free Mills & Boon Newsletter. If I choose not to subscribe I shall write to you within 10 days - I can keep the books and gifts whatever I decide. I can cancel or suspend my subscription at any time. I am over 18.

EP19D

Name (Mr/Mrs/Ms) _____

Address _____

_____

_____ Postcode _____

Signature _____

— MEDICAL ✚ ROMANCE —

The books for your enjoyment this month are:

ALL FOR LOVE Margaret Baker
HOMETOWN HOSPITAL Lydia Balmain
LOVE CHANGES EVERYTHING Laura MacDonald
A QUESTION OF HONOUR Margaret O'Neill

♥   ♥   ♥   ♥   ♥

Treats in store!

Watch next month for the following absorbing stories:

TENDER MAGIC Jenny Ashe
PROBLEM PAEDIATRICIAN Drusilla Douglas
AFFAIRS OF THE HEART Sarah Franklin
THE KEY TO DR LARSON Judith Hunte